CLAIMING HIS MATE

FATED MATES OF THE ATARI
BOOK 1

A.G. WILDE

PETRONIE PUBLISHING

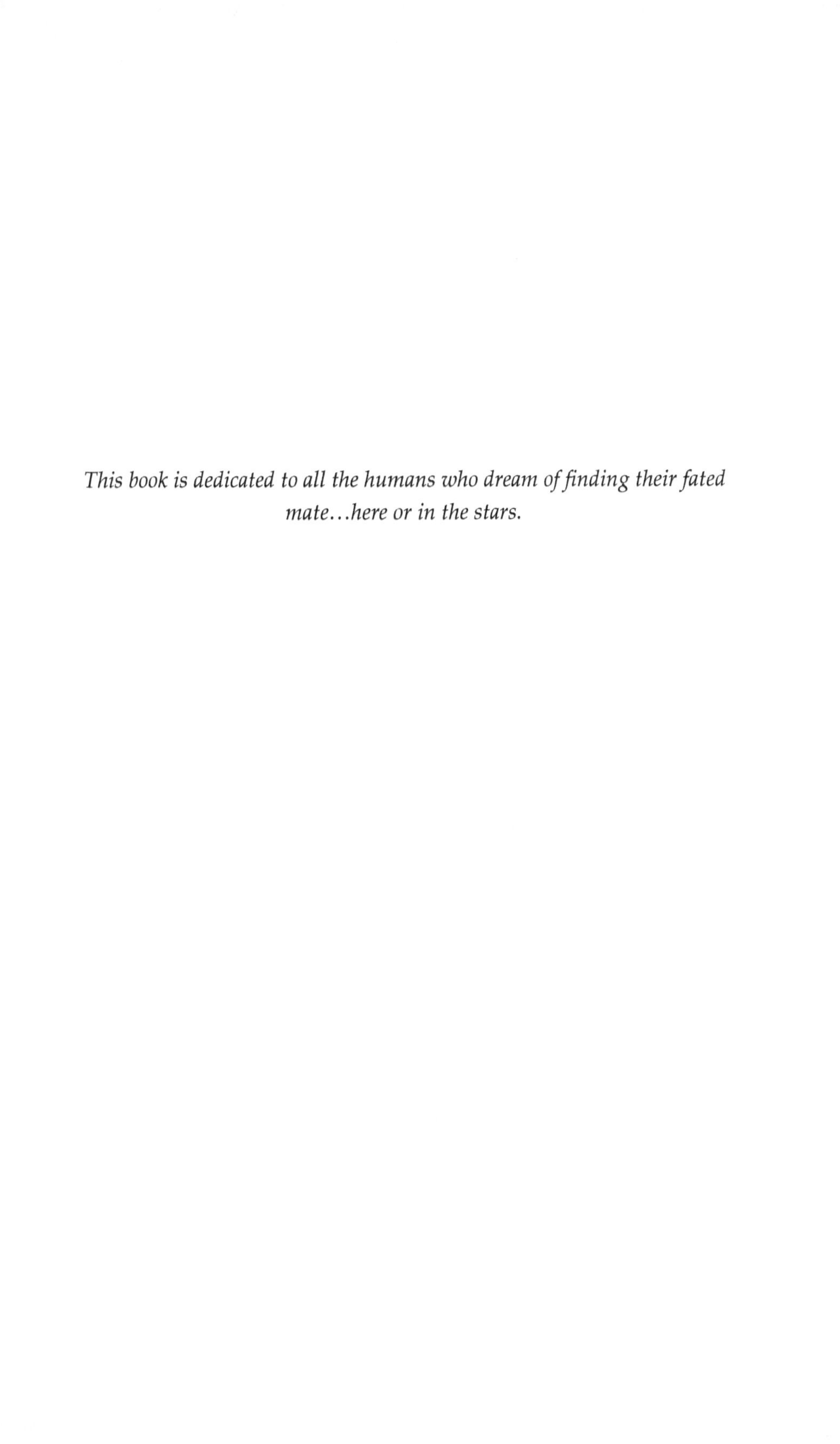

This book is dedicated to all the humans who dream of finding their fated mate…here or in the stars.

CLAIMING HIS MATE

When I get a once-in-a-lifetime chance to go on a luxury space cruise, I jump at it.

This cruise is the beginning of something amazing, and nothing is going to stop me from going.

But when things go wrong shortly after departure, it's clear I have made a mistake.

Suddenly thrown into a world where I have no way of defending myself, the last thing I expect is an Atari warrior coming to my rescue.

This cruise has been full of surprises…but the Atari is the biggest one of all.

He's tall, growly, possessive, and he sends my pulse into overdrive with just the slightest look.

Why the heck is my body reacting this way to this stranger?

And did he just declare that I am his mate?

1

Marion

My hand tightens around my ticket, almost crushing it as I enter the ship. There's no one to greet us at the entrance, and no staff waiting with smiles at the reception counter except for an old droid.

It scans my face and beeps, flashing green.

"Welcome, Marion Taylor. Your room is 5B. Please make your way to your quarters until the vessel ascends."

I grip the ticket tighter, my heart thumping with what could either be excitement or just rising anxiety.

Glancing behind me at the people waiting in line, I lower my voice, my cheeks warming.

"Um, wh-where are my quarters?"

I've never been on a cruise before, much less one touted as a luxury affair sponsored by the World Government.

Heck, I've never even been in a ship that went off-world before. I have no idea where "my quarters" are.

The droid creaks as it turns its head to the left to look down the corridor. It raises a metal arm and points.

"Follow the neon lights," it says, before turning to face me again.

"Thanks." I frown a little as it turns its attention to the woman behind me. Her eyes look right through me and my gaze falls to the white cane in her hand. It's one of the older models, from hundreds of years ago—as are most of the items from the lower levels. Like my dress and everything I own.

"Next," the droid says, and just like that, I'm dismissed.

My frown deepens.

For a luxury cruise, you'd think the government would at least put a droid that's newer, or better serviced, at the reception counter. Shaking my head, I push the thought from my mind as I turn away from the counter and begin walking down the corridor.

The hem of the long maxi dress I'm wearing brushes against my ankles in the cool breeze coming up from the floor vents, and I wrap my arm around my waist. It's chilly. I probably shouldn't have chosen a sleeveless dress.

As I go further into the ship, though, the breeze lessens, and soon I catch sight of the room numbers on the doors I'm passing.

5B. I'm 5B.

I scan the doors, but I'm currently passing level one, it seems. Other people are before me too, heading to their quarters as instructed. All women.

I glance back and the blind woman is about twelve feet behind me, heading down the corridor too.

Far behind her, a woman with crutches is at the droid's counter. I am yet to see any men.

Not that I mind. The less men the merrier.

Ahead, there is soft chatter and I realize some of the women must know each other from the outside.

I glance around. I don't know anyone here.

I wouldn't.

None of the people I know got an invitation to go on this cruise— few people get invites to go on free space cruises, period.

That's something only the upper, upper class has access to.

And that's why this is so hard to believe. That out of the many, many people on the ground, I was one of the government's top picks for this trip.

It's an amazing opportunity.

But as I head further into the ship, following the bright neon arrows showing me which direction to go in, I realize something else.

There's a woman in a wheelchair about nine feet ahead of me and when I glance behind me, the woman with crutches has caught up with the one using the cane.

She's using crutches to make up for the fact that she's missing a leg, but it doesn't seem to be a hindrance as she has no trouble keeping pace.

Self-consciously, I rub my stump and glance down at the space where the rest of my arm should have been.

It's always been that way, and no matter how hard I used to stare at it and wish it wasn't true, I couldn't run from reality. Not when born on one of the lower levels. Growing up with only one arm was my reality. One that I'd had no choice but to accept.

In front of me, the lady in the wheelchair stops at her room door, 4Z, and the corridor continues, curving upward.

"Damn. Just how many of us are on this cruise?" The woman with the crutches chuckles behind me. Her voice is rich and strong, melodious, and I turn and smile at her as I huff a laugh through my nose.

"Not very exclusive is it?"

I shake my head and we both chuckle.

"What room are you in?" she asks.

"5B," I reply. "You?"

She glances at her ticket. "5T."

"I'm 5P, I think," the woman with the cane says.

The corridor levels off again and we're finally on level five. At the end of the corridor, there doesn't appear to be a continuation, just a flat wall.

"Well, at least it doesn't continue going," says the woman with the crutches. "I'm Mona, by the way."

I nod. "I'm Marion."

"Rissa." The woman with the cane smiles.

My own smile brightens as I stop walking. My door is the second in line. "Guess I'll see you guys after we reach orbit?"

"Sure thing."

"Yeah, sure. We can explore this place together!"

I nod at them, still smiling.

The little conversation has me relaxing somewhat as I slide my ticket over the lock, and it clicks open.

A quick calculation in my head, though, tells me this cruise will have approximately one hundred and thirty participants.

That's a big cruise. Not something I thought the government would fund for free. According to the pamphlet, it's the first of its kind but not the last. With a new World President being sworn in only months before, this must be one of his initiatives.

Long have the social classes been so starkly separated, the state of the world economy and the strain on resources has been sorely evident. The lower class hardly got by, surviving with old technology and the meager resources trickled down from the upper levels.

The new president swore to fix that problem. That's why he won the election. For the first time in what feels like eons, a majority of the lower levels was able to vote. It had been an almost unanimous decision—the first of its kind in history.

The day he entered into office was the day new hope was breathed into the lower levels of New Earth.

It was the day I finally began looking forward to more than surviving. Things are going to get better. Life won't be so hard anymore, working and living hand-to-mouth. My disability won't be so much of a hindrance.

The barriers to moving up in society are about to be removed, and this cruise is the first evidence of that.

Taking a deep breath, smile still on my face, I push the door and enter my room. The light struggles to come on but when it finally does, I'm greeted with beige walls, a single cot attached to the wall, a stool, and a counter attached to the wall across from the cot. The room, or cabin rather, is suitable for a single occupant only.

That's fine. I'm here alone and I won't be spending much time inside it anyway. I plan to enjoy myself as much as I can before returning to the surface.

This is my first taste of what will be a new life, and I can't wait.

2

Marion

It takes forever for the ship to take off. Hours. And during that time, my door auto-locks and a message sounds over the intercom that we are to remain in our rooms.

With nothing to do, I flop on the cot and somehow doze off, only to be jolted awake when everything around me shakes.

For a moment, I'm blinking at the ceiling, wondering what the hell is happening, when the ship lurches again.

The lights in the room are dimmed. We must be finally heading into orbit...but shouldn't it be smoother than this?

New Earth's been traveling across the stars for many, many years, but my knowledge of space flight is limited to what I've read on the World Web.

People like me don't get to go up into orbit. This is all new and I have no idea what to expect. So when the ship jerks again I'm gripping the foam of the bed, wondering if something is wrong, if I'm overreacting, or if this is all...normal.

I get my answer soon after when the light flickers and becomes a little brighter and the shaking stops.

A droid speaks over the intercom. "Welcome to orbit. Your doors will now be unlocked. Please follow your maps to locate the toilets, washrooms, and meal hall."

There's a whirring-creaking sound and above the counter, slides a tablet from the wall. It stops when halfway out and jerks as if it is stuck.

Cursing under my breath, I slide off the cot and pull on the thing, dislodging it.

This ship really needs upgrading, but I won't complain. I have to count my blessings.

I have a few unsuccessful attempts of trying to turn the darn tablet on before the screen finally obliges.

The map comes up with a basic schematic of the ship.

The first thing I look for is the pool, but all I see are three areas: the toilets, the shower rooms, and, as the droid had said, the meal hall. Nothing else.

Strange…but I shrug it off and step toward the door.

I don't have a bag or anything. No belongings.

We were told to not bring anything with us, that everything—even clothing—would be provided free of charge. This cruise is supposed to be all-inclusive.

I assume those specific amenities will come later because the room I'm in is bare, apart from the meager furnishings.

With nothing else to do, I open my door and stick my head out, looking down the corridor.

Several women in conversation walk past and I search their faces for anyone I recognize. I catch the eyes of Mona and she waves at me. She's standing far down the corridor, having just exited her room. Closer to me, I see the tip of Rissa's white cane as she exits her room, too.

I step out of mine and head toward them, trying not to bump in the many other women heading in the opposite direction.

Their excited chatter fills the hall, and I can't help but be affected.

I'm beaming by the time I reach Rissa's side.

"Rissa," I say. "It's me, Marion."

The frown on Rissa's face disappears as she lifts her head and smiles my way. She's gripping her tablet and this time, she's donned dark shades to cover her eyes.

"Oh, hey," she says. "I was just about to head back into my room."

"Huh. Why?"

Her cheeks warm a little and she shrugs as if nothing is wrong. Her dark wavy hair shakes around her head. "Oh, nothing. Just thought I'd rest some more."

I'm happy she probably can't see my reaction because I'm frowning at her, wondering what the hell is wrong with her. We've been stuck in our rooms for hours. Anyone would want to leave.

But when my eyes fall on her tablet, I figure the reason why. How would she know where to go if the tablet isn't voice-activated?

Just to check, I lift mine and speak to it. "Zoom in."

Nothing.

I'd have to probably go to the settings to activate that feature and put on the voice navigation too. That means if I wasn't here, Rissa would be stuck, basically. There's no braille on the tablet screen. Nothing to make it accessible.

Granted, this is technology from the earlier times when Earth was still divided into countries with different governments. But even then, there were accessibility options.

This is a huge oversight by whoever organized this cruise. One of many if I'm going to count everything I've noticed so far.

"You guys ready?" Mona reaches our side and grins at us.

"Yeah." I nod and turn my attention back to Rissa. "You sure you wanna rest? You could always walk with us. I don't know anyone on this cruise, I sure would love the company." I try to add a bit of pleading to my tone. I wasn't lying about wanting company.

"Rest?" Mona laughs. "Girl, come on, let's go. You can rest later."

Rissa smiles and I can see her relief in the way her shoulders relax.

"As long as you two don't mind," she says.

"Of course, not!" Mona and I exclaim in unison.

We all giggle and a sense of comfort settles over me. I can already tell they'll be fun gals to hang with for the duration of this trip.

We can sit together by the pool, whenever we find it, and sip drinks and tell stories.

It will be the first time in a long while that I won't be worrying about taking any leisure time. Leisure interrupts any credits I earn, and days' off put me at risk of losing my shitty job as a bartender on the ground.

But none of that matters now. The World Government is paying for everything. My job is covered, and I can be free for just a little bit.

I'm going to enjoy every minute of it.

The walk to the meal hall is uneventful.

There's a gentle hum coming from the ship's engine that soon becomes background noise to our conversation.

I find out that Mona works—or worked, rather—with level cleanup. That's how she ended up losing her leg in a horrible accident with one of the machines.

Rissa's job is actually the coolest of us three. She's an artist and earns most of her income by selling her prints on the World Web.

They're all normal people, like me, and as we near the meal hall, I can't help but wonder why on Earth we were all picked for this cruise.

Mona echoes my thoughts as we enter the meal hall. It's packed with women of all ages. Some standing, some already seated. We manage to find a table with only one woman sitting there.

"Mind if we join you?" Mona asks.

I recognize the woman. She's the occupant of 4Z. I passed her just as she entered her room and I took the incline to the fifth floor.

She smiles at us and readjusts her wheelchair, gesturing to the three empty seats at the table.

"Of course, please sit."

As we sit, I allow my eyes to wander. "So many people," I murmur.

"So many *women*, you mean," Mona murmurs back. "I was hoping to meet a good man on this trip."

Rissa bursts out laughing, then stops promptly. "Sorry." Her cheeks grow red. "I can't tell if you're serious. It's just...I assumed you were joking."

"Why'd you assume I was joking?" Mona is serious and an uncomfortable air fills the table.

"I—I...sorry. I didn't think—" Rissa stutters just as Mona cackles loudly.

"Girl, I'm just messing with you. Ain't no such thing as a *good* man."

Her words make me and the other women burst out laughing.

"You're damn right about that." The woman in the wheelchair grins and Rissa lets out a relieved chuckle.

"I'm Trudy, by the way," she says. "What are your names?"

We all introduce ourselves and Trudy lets us know it's her first time on a ship like this, so it's a new experience for her.

"Mine too," I admit, and the others do as well.

"It totally surprised me when I got the e-vite. I almost marked it as spam," Rissa says.

"Same." Mona nods.

Trudy smiles before her smile dies and her gaze moves around the group of women in the room.

"I wondered why I was chosen," she almost whispers, "but I'm beginning to see why." She looks back at us. "At least, I *understand* why. Is this some sort of charity thing the government's going to be doing?"

We all go kind of silent, our eyes surveying the room.

Almost every woman in the room has some sort of visible disability.

I clear my throat and wait for one of the others to say something.

It's Mona who speaks first.

"Well, we all have something in common, that's for sure."

It seems we are all waiting for her to say it.

"We are hot as fuck."

There's a second where we all go silent, like we all hold our breaths, and then we're cackling like a bunch of old girlfriends. The laughter just about dies down when Rissa's stomach audibly growls.

"Sorry..." She cringes.

"No need to apologize," Mona says. "When are they going to feed us? I'm beginning to think the only luxury in this is their use of my time."

We all chuckle and as our little group continues small talk, I let my eyes wander around the room.

Maybe the president *is* turning things around for the disadvantaged of New Earth.

But why start with a cruise?

My thoughts are jarred the moment a loud alarm blasts through the meal hall, cutting off my every thought.

3

Marion

The alarm is so loud, I have to cover my ears.

"What the hell is that?!"

The others are just as confused as I am, and all the other women in the hall are either standing or sitting frozen, their eyes wide as we all scan the ceiling for the source of the alarm.

There is a deafening slam that jerks my flesh off my skeleton, and I almost jump out of my seat.

It's the doors to the meal hall.

There are two, one on each end of the hall, and they both slammed shut at the same time.

There is a loud click in the door closest to us, signaling the locking mechanism has been activated. I only hear because we're so close to the door itself.

My heart's slamming into my chest wall as I stand and walk over to the door. I push against it but of course it doesn't budge. It's automated.

"It's locked," I shout, turning to the girls at my table.

"What?" Trudy is wide-eyed as she shouts over the alarm. "That's strange. Maybe it's just a problem with this ship? It is kind of…"

"Trashy?" Mona shouts. "A piece of junk? You were going to say it's shit, right?"

Trudy shrugs.

"So we can't get out?" Rissa asks.

I shake my head before realizing she can't see me. "No!" I shout back. "We'll have to wait until the droids—"

"ALERT! ALERT! EMERGENCY EVACUATION NECESSARY. UNAUTHORIZED LIFEFORMS HAVE BOARDED THIS VESSEL. STATUS: HOSTILE."

I freeze completely as the alert is repeated over the intercom.

"ALERT! ALERT! EMERGENCY EVACUATION NECESSARY. UNAUTHORIZED LIFEFORMS HAVE BOARDED THIS VESSEL. STATUS: HOSTILE."

"ALERT! ALER—" The droid's voice becomes garbled and twists into unrecognizable sounds like the battery on a tape recorder dying.

It sounds ominous. Like the droid was just destroyed. Killed.

The tension in the meal hall suddenly rises and bursts into chaos.

Women stampede toward the doors, almost knocking me over as I push my way back to my table.

There's screaming. Shouting. A literal fight for life as every one of them tries to push against the doors.

Mona's on her feet, Rissa's extending her white cane, and Trudy is trying to maneuver her chair into a better position, but with the cacophony and movement of bodies around us, actually moving from the table is proving difficult.

"Did you hear that?" I ask stupidly. Of course, they heard it.

"Yes, but what the fuck does that even mean?" Rissa's sweet demeanor is filled with panic, and in another situation, her sudden curse would have made me doubletake, but I hardly even notice it.

"It means exactly what the droid just said." Mona's eyes are hard. "We're being hijacked."

"By who, though?" Trudy's hazel eyes are so filled with panic they shine back at me.

There are loud screams from the other end of the hall, causing us all to look that way and the horror of the sight in front of us has my organs shriveling into nothingness.

The doors to the hall are suddenly blasted inward, causing several of the women who were pressing against them to fly backward, their bodies crumpling like ragdolls.

One falls and hits the ground so hard, there's blood everywhere.

My hand instantly slaps over my mouth as the horror unfolds before me.

There's a scream close by and I don't know if it's Rissa, Trudy, or Mona, but I don't have time to look if they're okay. My eyes are focused on only one thing: the group of three aliens standing in the space where the door should have been.

There's that pause, where time stands still, and we stare at them as they stare back at us.

In the years since New Earth has taken to the stars, we've been contacted by several alien races. Aliens aren't new to us.

They leave us mostly alone but there are a few I know New Earth has alliances with.

These ones, though…I've never seen anything like them before.

Cold green eyes look back at us from hard armored faces. Layers and layers of spikes and horns grow from their heads.

They are bipedal, with long thick tails laying on the ground behind them.

I don't know what they are. All I know is that they're not friendly. In the next moment, they enter the room.

They move so fast, swinging long blades that slice through the women closest to the door.

As blood spills, coating the walls and the floor, the screams of the women are drowned out and I'm only jolted away from the terror when someone grips my arm.

Mona.

She's dropped one of her crutches to grab me.

"We have to get out of here!"

No need to tell me twice.

Grabbing Trudy's chair, I push her toward the door closest to us while Mona grabs hold of Rissa and does the same.

But there's no way to even get close to it.

The number of women there is like a human wall of writhing bodies all struggling to get through an impenetrable door. And the door's still locked.

"There has to be another way out of this room!" I shout, glancing behind me.

More blood.

More screaming.

The women at the other end of the hall are making their way toward us, but they're being cut down one by one.

Behind the aliens, not one person moves.

Not one body looks whole.

I choke down the lurch of my stomach and ignore the sudden weakness in my legs as I spin to face the slaughter.

There's only one way out and it's through the door that's been blasted open. Trouble is getting past the murderous beasts that are blocking the way, busy obliterating everything in their path.

Mona must realize the same thing because our gazes lock.

"What's happening?" Rissa asks.

"Trust me," I reply, "you don't want to know."

Rissa gulps and I know she can already tell from the screams that people are dying.

I nod at Mona and she returns the gesture. We have to try and get behind the aliens.

It will be a feat, but it is our only chance.

I turn, not second-guessing it as I push hard on Trudy's wheelchair, making a wide arch around the center of the room.

I hope the aliens don't see us. They seem intent on taking the lives of every person left and I have no doubt what will happen if they catch us.

The evidence, the blood…it's laid out in front of me.

I'm pushing Trudy's chair hard. My arm aches with the strain but I work with her as she manually pedals, trying to navigate through the throng of women running for their lives. I think we're making progress, even though it's a little, when I hear Mona's shout behind me.

I turn, and my heart falls. Rissa's tripped over a body, taking Mona with her.

I don't think about it twice. I let go of Trudy's chair.

"Try to get to the doors!" I shout to her.

Trudy nods and I don't wait as I turn and rush back toward Rissa and Mona.

They're struggling to stand while being trampled by the other panicked women and I get there just as someone falls over Rissa.

I manage to get Rissa into a sitting position and there's blood all over her face. Whether it's hers or someone else's, I don't know.

"Mona!" I shout Mona's name and it takes me a moment to find her in the flood of people around us. She's struggling to stand using her crutch and I scramble toward her just as there's a scream right above us. Hot liquid splashes right across my face.

I know it's blood. I can taste it in my mouth. But I don't want to acknowledge it.

I don't want to think about it.

I don't want to think that right above me, someone was just sliced—

But I don't get the chance to delude myself as the decapitated body falls right in front of me.

A scream lodges in my throat, my heart almost arresting as I hear the undeniable sound of sharp blades swishing through the air and cutting through more flesh.

It happens so fast.

Warm liquid rains down on me as bodies fall all around me.

I can only kneel and stare ahead in the horror that has me arrested.

And then…it is over.

The room is silent apart from the sound of my pulse thumping in my ears.

I want to think they're dead. That the aliens have somehow been killed by the security droids this ship *should* have.

But I know we're not so lucky when icy claws grip my arm and lift me upward.

I'm dangling in the air as I look straight into the cold green eyes of the hijacker.

I can't even move as his blade swings toward me. My vision blurs and I wait for the pain.

Nothing.

When my vision clears again, I see the blade inches from my belly, halted in midair.

"*Pakaa* no cargo." A voice says from the other end of the hall where the door's been blasted open.

It's another of the armored aliens, and a shiver goes through me. There are more of them out there. How many? I have no idea.

"No cargo?" The one holding me makes a sound I can't decipher the meaning of. "Then this trip *kekui* useless."

Galactic Standard. They're speaking the common language of the stars.

It's taught in schools on New Earth, but my handle on the language is less than stellar.

I can only understand some of what the aliens are saying.

"*Venkeshu* we should have *kanaa* that Kamia ship two rotations ago. *Palana kamui* much better *vendeshu*," says another.

It seems that in this moment of conversation, they've totally forgotten about us, and my eyes wander to the floor.

There is red everywhere. Bodies, everywhere.

But I catch sight of Rissa and Mona. I can tell they're alive, but neither is moving. Probably frozen in fear or playing dead.

I see Trudy's chair too, but she's no longer in it.

My heart lurches.

The alien holding me grunts. "What sort of cargo ship has no cargo?" he asks.

The other aliens remain silent as the one holding me pins me with his gaze.

I look straight back at him, fighting the shiver in my bones, fighting every response that threatens to show the fact I am scared out of my mind.

"Unless…" he says. There is a pause and my heart does another lurch as he lowers his weapon. "Maybe these *kezantha* things are the cargo. We should not have killed them all."

"We could not leave any observes."

Observes? No, that's not right. Observers maybe.

A chill goes down my spine.

Witnesses. They can't leave any witnesses.

The one holding me grunts.

"*Danaa.* But if this is the cargo, *bununo* we can still get some credits out of this trip."

One of the others makes a sound in his throat. "*Dakara!* That one isn't even whole. *Pavrenshi* its arm."

Shit.

The alien holding me turns me so it can look at me better and another shiver goes through me as its gaze drops to my nub.

The alien growls, a look of scorn growing in his eyes before he suddenly releases me.

I don't hit the floor. Instead, there's a sickening squelch as I land on the bodies littering the floor beneath me. My hand lands in something soft and I don't dare to look. That doesn't stop my empty stomach from trying to expel itself from my body, though.

As the alien walks away from me, I look up, confused.

They're sparing my life?

Because of my nub?

I don't understand, but my heart hammers as I watch him walk towards the doors that were blasted open.

I may yet survive this.

Wrong.

One of the other aliens approaches, blocking the light as he looms over me.

This time, instead of grabbing and lifting me by the arm, he takes a hold of one of my legs.

I scream and try to scramble away, kicking back at him, but my efforts are useless.

The last thing I see as I am pulled across the floor like a piece of trash, my body being dragged through the blood and gore the aliens have left behind, are the terrified eyes of Mona as she stares back at me.

4

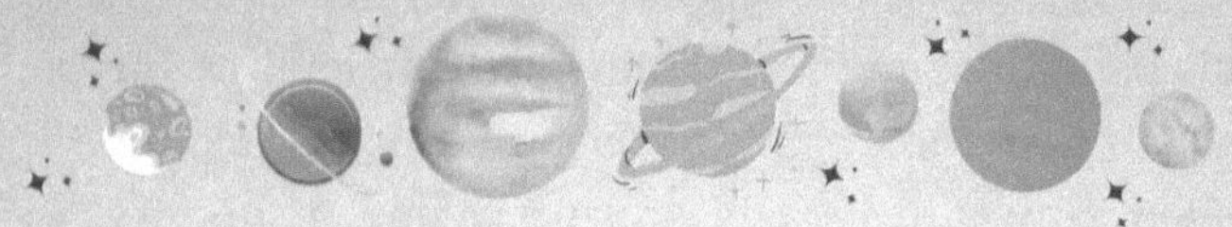

Aqnar

Our deal with the World Government of the planet Earth was already finalized. Then why is the ship with the females they gave us not where it's supposed to be?

A growl rumbles in my throat as I look through the viewscreen of our ship.

"Where is it?" Da'red, our prince and the Atari in charge of this expedition, squints at the viewscreen. "Do you think they changed their mind?"

"It would do us good. We never wanted the females anyway," Bhihan, third in command, leans closer.

On the other side of the control panel, Qhenno, fourth in command, searches through the schematics of this section of space.

"There's a weak signal coming off something close by. It might be them." He glances over at us.

"Or not," Bhihan growls. "I say we turn back. It's only out of desperation that we took this deal with the Earthkin, anyway. We needed the resources from their planet and they stuck us with this...*trap* to get rid of their own citizens. It is not our problem if they do not deliver." He looks over at Da'red, seeking approval to turn our cruiser around, but Da'red is silent.

I know what he is thinking. Although prince of our world, he is like a brother to me, and I know his heart is not as cold as Bhihan's.

"We head toward that signal," I say, leaning back in my seat. "If it is the female's ship, they may be in trouble."

Bhihan growls again. "We were supposed to meet them *here*, hook them up to our cruiser, and tow them back to Atari. We don't have time for a stupid rescue mission."

Da'red raises his hand, silencing Bhihan. His gaze focused on the viewscreen and the dark void out there.

"Aqnar is right," he finally says. "If it is the females, they might need our help. I doubt their government will aid them. The deal was for us to take them. If they are out there somewhere, they will be lost if we do not find them."

Bhihan curses under his breath before walking away and with a nod at Da'red, I fire up the engines once more.

"Qhenno," I say, "set navigation to the source of the signal."

Qhenno nods and soon, we are on our way.

Our ship is one of the best of Atar. Sleek. Fast. It doesn't take long before we arrive at the source of the signal and an old cargo cruiser comes into view.

I lean closer to the screen.

"Do you think that's them?" Da'red asks.

"It's an old cargo ship," I reply. I haven't seen one of that model in years. I didn't know those things would even be operable in this day and age. "Only one way to find out."

Rising from my seat, I head toward the back when a hand grasps my shoulder, stopping me.

"You can't go alone. We don't know if it's them," Da'red says.

He is right. But there are only four of us Atari on board. This was to be a simple pickup mission. If anything happens to me, Bhihan can take charge of flying the ship. We can't afford to lose Qhenno's navigation skills or the crown prince himself.

I am the best person to go out there.

I slap a hand on Da'red's shoulder. "I will be fine. It is but a simple check." I glance back at the viewscreen, my eyes narrowing a little. "The ship looks abandoned. It probably is."

This should only take a few minutes.

The small two-man space cruiser is almost too small to hold my frame. My knees are bunched up with the control wheel between them, but I manage to settle comfortably enough as I near the drifting cargo ship.

The lights are out. It looks dead, and I wonder if it is even worth it to board the vessel at all.

Whoever left it like this obviously is no longer on board.

Still, something pushes me to dock on the vessel and as my cruiser lands, no lights switch on to welcome my arrival.

Dead. Completely dead.

Grabbing a light core from the cruiser, I exit and the silence around me is deafening.

I can't see much, but the corridors are bare.

Years of being a guard in the Atari military come in handy though. I'm able to walk silently down the halls. All the doors so far are locked.

It's not till I reach farther into the ship that the smell hits me.

I stop in my tracks.

It's a sickeningly sweet smell. One that prompts me to guide my light from the roof straight down to the floor.

At first, the thick red streaks across the floor look like some sort of paint, but as I crouch and dip my finger into it, it comes off on my skin, coating my fingers.

I bring it to my nose and the sickening scent grows stronger.

Lifeblood.

I freeze, my ears perking.

This ship wasn't abandoned. Something catastrophic happened here.

Switching off my light, I choose to walk in the darkness, relying on my senses alone.

It doesn't take me long to follow the sweet scent till I reach a wide entrance and I pause.

It is the only door that's open and my fingers brush over where the hinges should be only to be greeted with a jagged edge.

Blasted off with great force.

The sickening scent is strong in this room. So much so that I'm tempted to turn away from it, but there is still no sound.

It is too dark for me to see what is inside.

I have no choice but to switch my light on once more and as soon as I do, the horror before me is revealed.

Bodies.

More than I can count.

Lifeblood…everywhere.

I step into the room, stepping over one of the bodies, and crouch to look more closely at it.

A soft face greets my gaze. Skin so pale, I can see the network of veins beneath.

Female.

Her eyes are open. The horror of her last moments captured in her still gaze.

I recognize the species immediately.

Human.

I have visited their planet enough to know them at first glance and the realization hits hard.

The human females we were supposed to pick up. This is their ship. And they have all been…

I rise, shining my light around the room.

All of them. Dead.

Not one remains alive. Not one moves.

Decapitated in a most vicious of attacks.

Only one race kills so viciously. The Khuru.

The fact that none of the females were left alive supports that too. The Khuru never leave any witnesses behind.

Fek.

Activating the communication panel on my arm, I ping our ship.

Qhenno answers immediately.

"Find anything?"

"Yes."

"What?"

"I have found the females."

He breathes out a breath of relief. Unlike Bhihan, Qhenno had been looking forward to meeting the females…to potentially finding a mate in one.

"Okay, I'll dock the cruiser and attach the tow line. Looks like they ran out of power?" he asks.

"No," I reply.

"What do you mean?" Da'red takes the communicator. "Why are they drifting without lights?"

I only have to say one word. "Khuru."

There is silence on the other end of the line before someone curses. "Fek."

"Return to the cruiser," Da'red finally says. "We must divert to Earth. Tell their government what happened. It's the least those females deserve."

"Understood," I reply.

My boots make squelching sounds as I walk from the room and my facial muscles strain so hard, it takes me a moment to realize I am scowling.

Innocent females. Abandoned by their government, and now killed by bloodthirsty criminals.

I grip the light core in my hand. I want to punch something.

A Khuru, if I could.

The rage inside me is building so much that I almost don't hear the soft knock against one of the locked doors.

I stop in my tracks, my head turning slowly toward where I heard the sound, and then I hear it again.

Something or someone is still alive on this ship.

Bracing against the door, I push hard. It doesn't budge.

It's going to take more force, but I am Atari. Nothing will stand in my way.

Taking a few steps back, I rush forward, slamming my body into the door.

The sound ricochets down the corridor, but I am no longer cautious of making the occupants of the ship aware of my presence.

If the Khuru were still on board, I would have known already. They never stay long when they hijack a ship.

Whatever is behind this door could be a female.

"Stand back!" I shout as I take a few steps backward and launch myself at the door once more.

It creaks, bending inward, and I use my foot to kick it open. It goes flying inward to reveal a dark room.

Shining my light in, I search the darkness for the female, but all my light lands on is the upper body of an old droid.

Its arm rises and falls to the floor before it does the action again.

A fekking droid. Cursing underneath my breath, I walk toward it.

It's an old model. One that's been decommissioned on most worlds.

I pull my gaze from it and glance around.

This is a security room.

If there were security droids, why do I not see any Khuru casualties?

Unless…

"Fek," I curse again.

When the Earth government forced this deal on us, I thought they were scum. But this makes it even worse. They didn't even outfit the ship with security droids.

The one on the floor is just a basic model that was used for simple tasks.

If this is all that was on the ship to protect the females, no wonder I witnessed the massacre in that room.

The females had no chance.

Walking over to the panel with the security controls, I initiate the security feed. It comes up with words I cannot read. Earthspeak.

I curse again before glancing down at the droid.

Crouching, I lift the metal body and point the droid at the security panel.

"Access the security feed and change the language to Galactic Standard," I command it.

"Authorization needed," the droid replies, its voice glitching in and out.

I'm tempted to chuck it to the floor.

"Under authority of Prince Da'red of the Atari in treaty with the Earthkin World Government."

I raise an eyebrow at the thing, not sure what I said will work, but its eyes flash green before its working arm reaches forward and types a code into the control panel.

It's not long before I can read the words on the screen and I put the droid down.

Navigating the security system is easy. There are no inbuilt restrictions and soon I'm pulling up the feed of the last few hours.

My eyes burn red as I watch the Khuru board the ship. Their armored bodies are easy to distinguish. A ruthless race that has no home in our galaxy, they raid the undefended and take their spoils to build their empire.

I watch as they take easy control of the ship before finding the room where the women were hidden.

I am frozen as I watch the massacre unfold. Only a creature with no life organ can do such a thing to another.

One after the other, the women are cut down. I am a warrior. I have seen many deaths. But the deaths of innocents...I almost turn away from the footage.

And then I see her. She's covered in blood. The light-colored garment she wears clings to her body as she pushes another female who is bound to a chair with wheels.

I wonder what she is doing, and I find my gaze fastening on her instead of the Khuru on the screen.

Short dark hair that stops just above her shoulders swings as she whips her head, her incredibly light-colored eyes shining with fear.

All the other females are running toward the back, while she is heading toward the violence. I don't understand until I see where her eyes are focused.

The doors that were blasted inward.

My life organ thumps. I want her to make it. I want her to survive even though I already know how it ends.

But something stops her in her tracks.

The footage has no sound, but I see when her wide eyes turn, and she looks behind her. She shouts something to the female in the chair before doubling back through the chaos.

A Khuru swings his blade at her, it only misses her because she suddenly ducks. That same blade slices the head off another woman.

Lifeblood rains down and I search the sea of women, dead and alive to catch sight of the one with the light eyes.

I see her in the next second when she grabs another woman on the ground. While, everyone around her is dying, she is taking the time to help another. Her instincts to save herself...they are nonexistent.

I am entranced by her as she gets the other woman into a sitting position before she turns and screams something, her eyes searching the sea of death.

The lifeblood spattered across her face is like a strange painting and I find I cannot look away.

Frozen in terror, she searches the sea of bodies for something—or someone.

That's when the massacre ends. A Khuru grabs her by the arm and a growl rumbles in my throat at the fact.

I don't know this female, but I do not want to watch her die.

Still, I cannot look away.

I watch the exchange, right till she is thrown to the ground and another Khuru takes hold of her by the leg, pulling her through the sea of death around them.

I switch the camera perspective, following them through the corridor, my life organ thumping in my chest, right until I see the Khuru throw her into a cruiser.

She...she is alive.

I blink at the screen, not believing what I just witnessed.

The Khuru never leave survivors.

There's only one reason they would have taken the female. To sell her...or to keep her for themselves.

Both options are as terrifying as the other.

Slaves are outlawed in this galaxy. Anyone who buys this female will be doing so for nefarious reasons.

I don't think twice about it

I have to go after her.

Save her.

I almost miss the other Khuru also boarding their separate cruisers with one…two…three other females.

Four females survived this ordeal.

I have to—no—*we* have to save them.

Racing from the room, I head to my cruiser, instincts I long thought I buried coming to the fore.

I am an Atari warrior and I have felt a new taste for blood. These Khuru will not go unpunished.

5

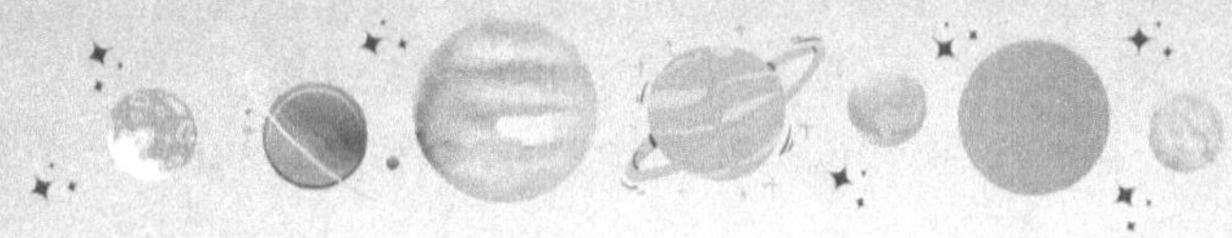

Marion

My whole body aches as I struggle against the restraints.

I'm in some kind of small ship and we're moving fast.

There is a single murderer in front of me, sitting in the pilot's seat.

After tying my legs together, he tied my arm to a part of the ship itself and has paid me no mind since he's done so.

I don't want any attention, but it's clear he has some plan for me.

I can't imagine what it is. Not after what I just witnessed. Not after what just happened.

I choke on air as my heart swells in a most uncomfortable way. A cramp goes through my chest.

I'm covered in blood and guts. Caked in it, and the smell makes my stomach turn.

What had we done to deserve this? What had all those innocent women done to die like they did?

And…why was I spared?

Guilt consumes me as I think of the three women I made friends with.

After the alien pulled me from the room, I didn't see what

happened to them. If they survived, if they're still alive, I hope they get back to New Earth somehow.

But even as I think this, I know that hope is far from the true reality.

I stare at the alien in front of me, tears in my eyes that I refuse to let fall.

My wrist burns with the effort I've made to release myself. Yet, still I try, only startled when a voice sounds on the ship.

It's in a language I don't recognize and the alien before me speaks back to it. He makes a low growling sound as his shoulders rise and fall and it doesn't take me long to realize he is laughing.

Laughing…after killing so many innocents without a second thought.

Anger rises within me.

"What do you want?" I ask in Standard.

The alien freezes and I'm suddenly once again aware of his size and power.

He turns to glance behind him, cold green eyes settling on me.

"This one can speak Standard," he says so I can understand, and the communicator in the ship crackles.

"Sell it for twice the credits then," his accomplice says.

Again, there's that low extended growl as the alien's shoulders quake.

My anger spikes once more.

"Who are you…going to…sell me to?" I have to pause between words as my brain figures out how to put the sentences together. I only know Standard because there was a free course that New Earth's government had offered in the early days of us encountering aliens.

It's been a long time since then. I've had no need to speak it regularly and it's clear I'm rusty.

"The highest *granietsu*," the alien replies.

I do not know what *granietsu* means.

"When?" I ask, but the alien turns back around and begins ignoring me again. I press my lips together, but I know I'm lucky he even entertained any of my questions in the first place.

Gritting my teeth, I continue trying to get my arm out of the restraint.

It's all I continue doing until the ship starts to descend.

I see a planet below, one I have no idea the name of, and as we near it, huge metal structures rise from the ground into the sky.

The ship swerves around them easily, despite the thick fog...or smoke...that fills the air.

I push back the fear rising within me, my eyes searching the view for anything remotely familiar. But all I see are the towering brown buildings.

As we get closer, I spot the large funnels atop the buildings. Huge plumes of smoke rise from within them.

Factories.

This is a manufacturing city.

On New Earth, knowledge of what lies beyond is scarce for those of us who live on the lower levels. Information itself is scarce. Education isn't something that is stressed.

Only the upper class know what civilizations lie out here, so I can't imagine what's on the ground.

I want to think the people on this planet are honorable workers. Good people.

But from the scumbag in front of me, those hopes die quickly. The old saying of birds of a feather flock together and all that. He's not carrying me to anyone who has got any sort of high moral compass. That's for sure.

It's not long before the ship lands and the murderer switches the engine off. His tail slaps against the cold floor, causing me to jerk as he rises and turns toward me.

I don't meet his gaze. Instead, I keep staring forward, my eyes pointed at his armored chest.

Even if I get a weapon and try to stab him, I doubt the blade would go through.

Without a word, he reaches over me, grabbing my arm so hard I wince as he releases the restraint from whatever he tied it to.

Grabbing the other end of the cord, he pulls me into a standing position, and an upward glance catches him giving me a once-over.

The fact he is looking at me while so close makes a chill go down my spine. But he grunts and says nothing before the door of the ship opens and he steps out.

Not waiting for me to even begin walking, he yanks on the cord that's around my wrist, pulling me behind him.

I have to hop since my legs are still tied.

"You can at least cut the cord around my legs." It's not like I could run away anyway with him holding my wrist hostage.

But the murderer doesn't care.

He ignores me and continues walking forward.

I hop in quick succession, but there is no way I am going to keep up with his pace. Not like this.

I fall to the hard ground, my head hitting the side of a rock, and my vision blurs for a moment.

There's a growl as my wrist is tugged again and I struggle to rise, but my head swims.

I can't.

There's another growl before a searing white line of heat erupts across my back.

I choke on the pain, unable to scream.

The whip cracks in the air before it lands on my back once more. I can only squirm as I try to roll away from the onslaught, a deep inhale arresting my lungs as pain erupts across my spine.

The whip cracks again and I feel when it eats through my skin, cutting the fabric of my dress to burn into my flesh.

Tears flood my eyes as my body spasms and I let out a pained cry.

I barely hear the murderer growl something before he stomps closer, gripping me by the neck as he pulls me to my feet.

Even with the pain blurring my vision, I see his cold green eyes on me, and at this moment I know: I've never hated anything in my life the way I hate this beast before me now.

The alien removes a blade from his waist and I grip the claw he has around my neck.

There's fresh blood in my mouth, my own this time, and somehow my lip twists into a smile.

Even if he kills me now, this bitch is going to pay. If I have to come back from the grave to make sure he does, then so be it.

But the knife doesn't get buried into my belly. Instead, the alien swipes down and my legs suddenly dangle free.

He's cut the restraints holding my ankles together.

He drops me then and pulls on the lead holding my wrist once more.

I struggle to stand but somehow make it to my feet.

My entire body feels like it's on fire, but I have no time to adjust. He's pulling me again and this time, I stagger behind him.

I can barely see the details of our surroundings as he continues pulling me relentlessly. All I know is the dirt here is dry, yet the air is thick, the atmosphere humid.

There are loud sounds all around us—machines banging metal against metal and the sound of many, many voices.

It's not long before we are surrounded by people—aliens.

I try to look around, to get my bearings, but it is difficult in this throng.

The crowd moves quickly, as if everyone is on some sort of business here.

I'm pushed and bumped into, my body swaying as I try to keep up with the alien leading me. The only thing keeping me on my feet is the strong hold he's got on the cord around my wrist.

There are many different types of aliens around us. Not just one species like I thought it would be. This is not just one civilization.

My gaze flicks from one alien to the other and what I see only increases the fear crawling over my spine.

None of them look kind. Their eyes are shifty. Cold. And they're all mostly dirty, their clothing turned dark brown and black from what must be hard work in the factories.

Those who *do* make eye contact with me turn to stare, their gazes curious. But they all continue on.

No one stops to ask the murderer leading me what he's doing or why he's got a woman restrained and being pulled behind him.

No one looks surprised either.

It must be common here.

A little part of me dies inside.

I am on my own.

I've been on my own for a long time. But even in the dark streets of New Earth's lower levels, I've never been more afraid of that fact.

I find myself staring at each and every alien that meets my gaze, this fact cementing in my brain when the murderer tugs me mercilessly.

I almost stumble but manage to pick up the pace.

He hasn't killed me yet. He obviously has plans for me.

He takes a sharp right, pulling me through the crowd and into an alleyway between two large dirty metal buildings.

The stench down this road is so strong, I wish I had use of my hand so I could cover my nose.

Pungent ammonia wafts up from the ground and the only thing protecting my feet from the urine is the flimsy slip-ons I'd worn to go on the stupid cruise.

Fuck.

Does the government even know something happened to us? Surely, they were monitoring the ship. Surely, they know something terrible has happened. Surely, they sent help.

Hope flares within me for a moment. Hope that maybe I will be found. Hope that maybe this nightmare will end soon.

But I'm nowhere near the ship and after what happened there…it's safe to assume the World Government will think every woman on that cruise is now dead.

I gulp back a sob at this fact as I struggle to keep up with the murderer. There's no telling what my future holds.

Bright light almost blinds me as we exit the alley. But the sun is soon hidden again as the murderer turns sharply and begins going downward.

The stairs are narrow, just wide enough to walk single file, and the lower we go, the stronger the scent of dampness and mold.

Soon, the stairs stop in front of an unmarked, metal door.

The alien knocks and I try to see around him, but he's so large he blocks my view.

"Where are you taking me?"

Turning so quickly his tail almost whips me across the midsection, the alien closes the short distance between us and grabs my lower jaw, causing my lips to twist as he squeezes my face.

His grip is painful but I'm more terrified by the cold look in his eyes.

"You remain quiet unless spoken to," he growls.

I don't reply, and after a few seconds, he releases me just as the door behind him opens.

The alien on the other end is yet another race that has not yet visited New Earth, to my knowledge.

He is a mass of lumps and folds—more like a sentient glob than anything else. I am not sure where his head ends and his body begins.

He eyes the murderer before his gaze slips to me.

They say nothing, as if they already had a conversation beforehand, and before I know it, I'm being pulled into a dark room.

It takes a few moments for my eyes to adjust to the scene before me.

Several cages, some already occupied, are hanging from the ceiling in a large, otherwise empty room.

My gaze flicks from one cage to another and the terrified eyes of those caged look back at me. Dried tears are on some of their faces. Some don't even need tears—the sorrow is almost tangible in their eyes.

Some are bloody, others dirty.

As I'm pulled further into the room, there is a creak and a cage slowly lowers. Without a word, the murderer yanks on my lead, pulling me toward the lowering cage. In a panic, I glance back at the door we entered through, watching as it closes slowly, shutting out my hope and prayers for help.

A moment ago, I wasn't sure what was in store for my future, but as the cage lowers before me, it becomes as clear as day.

I'm about to be sold into slavery…and everyone knows, the survival rate for those who fall into the underground slave ring is next to zero.

I'm doomed.

6

Aqnar

I barely manage to send a coherent message back to our main cruiser.

There is no time to waste.

Knowing the Khuru, there are a number of places where they would go to dispose of illegal slave victims and waiting too long could be to the detriment of the females.

Da'red gave the order as soon as I told him what I saw on the security feed. There's no time to contact New Earth, so we have to do this ourselves.

We'll go after the females, try to find them. Try to rescue them.

I'm already on my way.

The closest planet to our current location is one called Ockorius III. It's a dirty factory pit filled with thieves, murderers, and petty criminals.

It's the perfect place to get rid of a slave—either by getting them to work in one of the factories or by other means.

It's my best bet, so I head there first.

Even before I land, my nostrils flare with disgust at the sight of the surface.

I've only been to this planet twice before, both times against my will, but through duty to the Atari military.

I have no friends here. On this world, I doubt *anyone* has friends.

I hope that works in my favor.

Docking at the ship bay, I hop out, concealing my blade and blaster underneath the oversized robe I don to hide my features.

The attendant hurries over to me, a devilish gleam in his eyes as his gaze skims over my cruiser. He'll have it scrapped for parts as soon as my back is turned no doubt.

"Take care of it," I say to him, flipping a Galactic credit into the air toward him.

His beady eyes widen and his mouth opens, an unhidden drool falling from his lips as he grabs the coin greedily.

"Make sure it's like this when I return, and I'll double the payment."

The attendant is nodding eagerly, both hands gripping the credit as if he is afraid I will snatch it away from him.

"It will be in perfect condition…master." He pauses, eyeing me. His head dips a little as he tries to see underneath the hood of my cloak. "I will even wash it for you. I have a special wax that will keep the exterior well preserved during takeoff to orbit."

He beams at me.

"No need," I grunt, brushing past him.

He says something else that I don't care to hear as my focus turns to my surroundings.

There are several places in this city where a female could be sold.

One so soft and small would most likely not draw the attention of the factory overseers. But for other, more twisted beings, I know exactly what they would see her being best used for.

I have to move. And fast.

The throng of factory workers moving to and from their jobs is one that reeks of blood, sweat, and toil. Most of these beings are repaying debts they had no choice but to be laden with. Some had their homes taken away, their families imprisoned, all because they made the wrong choices.

It's why the general mood is bitter in this place.

No one on Ockorius III is happy. None content.

And that means… with the right amount of credits, they can be easily bought.

Walking along the side of the road, I keep my head bent, my eyes on the lookout for any lonely soul who might give me some information.

I see my target not long after.

He's old. Crouching. His robes ripped and dirty. He sits on a small boulder by the side of the road, watching everyone go by. He has the eyes of a being that has seen many things, but to others, he might look like just a poor vagrant.

I approach him and stop when I am standing right beside him.

He does not acknowledge my presence and I say nothing.

Without a word, I slip a galactic credit between my fingers and lower my hand enough for him to see the glint of the golden metal.

I sense when he sees it because he shifts a little. His mouth opens and his double tongues flick over his lips.

"I want to buy something," I speak low.

"I have nothing to sell," he replies.

"Information," I say.

He licks his lips again. "What do you want to know?"

"A slave. I need one."

His shoulders shake a little as he grunts. "Many places to get those here. Don't need to spend a galactic credit to find out where."

He is right. If I want a worker, I simply have to walk up to anyone on the street and offer them more payment than their current employer.

"A special type of slave," I reply. "One that can fulfill my…needs." I almost choke on the word, and it leaves a nasty taste in my mouth.

He grunts again. "Ah," he says. "That information deserves a galactic credit."

"Do you know where I may find what I need?"

He nods and opens his palm to me.

I drop the credit into his hand and it promptly disappears under his clothing.

"Follow the road. Keep to the right. Take the alley. Then the stairs."

He goes back to ignoring me and I walk away, repeating the instructions in my head.

It's not long till I reach the alley.

It reeks of excrement, and I quicken my steps. I've never liked the sleazy underground of Ockorius III.

The alley was easy to find. The stairs, though, I almost miss.

They're concealed between two buildings and, at first, they look like a dark hole.

Barely wide enough for me to fit through without brushing against the walls; I head down them till I reach a door.

Glancing behind me, I note the silence.

This has to be the place.

One rap on the door and more silence. I'm about to rap again when it creaks open and a Zedice stands before me.

Just the sight of him and I know I am at the right place. It is widely known that the Zedice's preferred form of business is the illegal dealings of trafficked beings.

It is unusual to see one walking above ground. Their kind prefers to dwell in the underground, seeping between the cracks and depressions underneath the surface.

The Zedice looks me up and down, his body rippling as his head moves.

"What business do you have here, stranger?" His voice is deep, rumbly, and almost too low to hear.

"I am here for the sale."

He dips his head, trying to see under my cloak, but I don't move to reveal myself.

"You must be mistaken. I do not sell anything here."

I know he lies.

"I've been told this is the place to acquire the rarest of…items," I say to him, tilting my head a little so he can see my eyes.

His widen somewhat. "An Atari," he whispers, and he takes a step backward. "I'm afraid you are mistaken, warrior."

He moves to close the door but I'm faster than he can move. My boot prevents the door from closing.

"I'm sure you don't want to turn down what I'm offering." I lower my voice and hold up my bag of credits, shaking them so he can hear the coins tinkling. "It would be a pity to lose out on a customer willing to pay."

He doesn't look convinced. "Your kind does not buy what I sell," he says.

He is right. No Atari would find themselves buying a trafficked being.

They would rather cut their hands off and those of the seller before stooping to such levels.

I make a show of returning my coin bag to the hidden folds of my cloak.

"You do not know my kind as well as you think." I turn slightly.

"Pity," I continue. "I had word that you have a new specimen I was quite interested in." I pause, letting the words settle. "You are right. I must have been mistaken."

I turn my back to him and take a few steps away, heading back to the stairs.

My life organ thumps. I need him to stop me. I need him to let me in willfully. That would make things much easier because I need to see inside. I need to check if she is here.

If he doesn't let me in, I will kill him.

As I hoped, though, his voice stops me in my tracks.

"How much are you willing to spend today, friend?"

Friend now, am I?

I turn, a soft smile on my lips. "As much as it takes."

***

Marion

The room slowly fills up. More slaves are put into cages and more people—aliens—fill the room below.

I watch them keenly. None of them look like the dirty workers I walked past above ground.

These aliens are cleaner. They don't walk hunched. Their hands and claws aren't caked with dirt, and their whole demeanor tells me they are far better off than the aliens working in the factories.

I keep my eyes on them, studying each one, and my cage shakes slightly with every movement I make.

I will belong to any one of these aliens in a short time and none of them, not one, looks remotely kind.

Like the other unfortunates in cages around me, I continue watching the aliens below as the room continues to fill.

Those below us walk slowly beneath our cages, eyes upward as they scan the wares on display.

My eyes catch those of an almost humanoid one. His skin is green and there is a slight sheen to it as if he has soft scales.

He doesn't have nasal cartilage like humans do. Instead, there are simply two dark holes in the middle of his face and his ears are also shorter than a human's.

He notices me looking at him and his eyes brighten.

I don't know whether that is a good or bad thing, but he doesn't look as bad as some of the other buyers here.

If anyone gets me, I hope it is him. Though the thought makes a horrible feeling go through my belly. Trading one demon for another…

Just because he looks nice doesn't mean he isn't cruel.

My heart sinks further when more buyers enter the room.

They seem to be arriving randomly but as the room fills, it's clear that the event will start soon.

There is hardly enough space on the floor now for them to stand without bumping into each other.

That fact only makes my heart beat harder.

Finally, the moment of truth arrives.

The huge alien that mans the door glides to the center of the room and speaks in a language I do not know.

He gestures to the cages and there is a low, excited wave of whispers that rolls across the group.

"Our first hu-bli today," he says, switching to Standard as he gestures up toward the cages.

My heart lurches but my cage doesn't move.

Instead, one to my far right is slowly lowered and the being inside of it scrambles to the front, gripping the metal bars, fright in his eyes.

He is small, about three feet, and thin. He is hairless and ears too big for his head are pressed back flat against his skull, a signal of his distress. Wearing only something to cover his privates, I can see his ribs poking through his upper body.

His head shakes, sharp little inhales racking his body. His gaze flicks from one buyer to another as his cage is lowered to hang right above the alien running the sale.

"Two *granietsu*," the seller says.

Again, that word. I can only assume it is referring to money.

Credits.

No one in the crowd says a word.

"One and half credit." The seller lowers the price.

Still, no one makes any indication they are willing to buy what he offers.

"One credit."

No one replies.

"Half credit."

Nothing.

The seller shifts and the cage with the little alien rises slowly once more.

"Closed," the seller says.

I blink down at the crowd and the seller, confused.

"Oh no!" The little alien suddenly speaks. "No! Please! I will work hard. Very hard. I will do anything you want!"

Some of the buyers shift their eyes away and the little alien begins shaking the bars of his cage.

"Please!" He begins pleading some more, his words coming out so quickly I can't follow with my limited grasp of the language.

"He belongs to the Zedice now," the alien closest to me says.

From the hair, I assume it is a female. Long dark strands cover most of her face and she turns four startling blue eyes my way.

She is beautiful.

I have no doubt she will get bought.

"What do you...mean?" I whisper. "What is the...Zedice?"

She glances down and gestures to the seller. "They are not kind *jusirs*," she says. "Many die within the first rotation with a Zedice. You will do better sold."

My mouth goes dry.

As if I didn't have enough problems, I have to worry about actually being bought? I thought that was a sure thing.

My gaze flicks with renewed panic over the group of buyers below.

Fuck. Fuckity fuck fuck.

Self-consciously, I try to wipe away some of the blood from my face, but it's already dried. My efforts do nothing. And, as I'm doing this, I catch sight of my missing arm.

New fear spikes through me.

As the murderer and his friends had said, *I am not whole.* They almost killed me because of that. To them, I almost wasn't worth the trouble.

As I scan the group below, I find myself turning so my nub isn't in plain view.

It makes me feel like shit, hiding the fact about myself.

As a kid, I'd learned the hard way to accept myself for who I am… but what happens now when that fact might get me killed?

I can't take the chance.

I have to survive this.

I have to come out of this alive.

7

Aqnar

There are several cages suspended above. More than I expected.

Unfortunate beings stare down at us, fear in their eyes.

Most defeated.

Most pleading with their gazes.

Standing below them, looking at their plight, I cannot stop the rage building within me.

The Zedice's operation is unlawful. *Illegal.*

No being should be subjected to this.

As the first unfortunate being is lowered and the Zedice begins the bids, the silence is almost overwhelming.

It's a *newot*. A race of small beings that are often used as house help.

This one must have been abandoned by his previous employers for some less than stellar reason.

That is unfortunate…because newots usually bond with one family, and one family only, working with them for life. They take care of the family's dwelling while the family provides food, board, and protection. It's an almost symbiotic relationship, with most families treating them as if they are tied to them by blood.

Because of this, it is unlikely for a newot to bond to another employer. He will be loyal to no other, even when the bond is broken. For a newot to be sold on the underground…

I am not surprised when not one buyer around me puts in a bid for the unfortunate creature. Its cries as it is pulled away, only increase the anger brewing within me.

My gaze flicks across the group of beings in the cages and at first, I do not recognize the human.

My gaze slides past her, a frown creasing my brow as I wonder whether I have made a mistake coming to this place. If she is not here…finding her will take much longer and be more difficult.

It is not till they pull the newot's cage past hers that I finally spot her.

She is almost unrecognizable.

Grime and filth coat her skin, covering its light color like a dark haze. Her dark hair is clumped together, her garments torn and hanging…

The only things I recognize are the same eyes that looked back at me on the security feed.

At the realization, relief surges through me and I take a step forward from my position at the back of the group.

She is sitting awkwardly, one side turned toward the group of buyers, and one arm gripping the cage as she looks down at us.

Like the others in her situation, there is fear in her eyes, but there is also something else.

Unlike the pleading gazes of the beings around her, the human's gaze flicks across the group of buyers with calculation.

She eyes each and every one below her for a few seconds before her gaze moves to the next, as if she is trying to work out who they are, or *what* they are.

I notice when her gaze slides to a *velushan* that is standing with his back against the wall. More than once, her gaze finds its way back to him. And his focus is on her too. As a matter of fact, she is the only prisoner he's focused on.

The thick row of scales at the back of his head pulse in anticipation.

He wants her.

And I know exactly for what.

Velushans may share similar physical traits to the Atari, but one thing separates us—we don't forcefully impregnate females to bear our young, killing them in the process.

It is a vicious cycle, one I am sure will happen if I let him get his claws on the human.

He must sense my scorching gaze, for his gaze shifts from the human for the first time and finds mine immediately.

We stare at each other for several slow seconds.

He's not getting her.

She is mine.

"And now, this...lovely item," the Zedice announces. "A creature that will be good for many uses..." The Zedice pauses. "...once it is given a good clean."

There is a chuckle from one of the buyers and the soft gasp of the female as her cage is lowered is the only thing that pulls my gaze away from the velushan.

As she is lowered, I get a better look at her.

She is small.

Smaller than I thought.

She will reach no higher than my chest if I put her to stand before me.

Before her cage is lowered enough for all buyers to see, the velushan speaks.

"Ten creditssss."

The Zedice's eyes bug out. It's clear he was going to start with a much lower amount.

The human's eyes are wide too as her gaze darts to the velushan. She blinks at him, her throat moving as her chest heaves with huge breaths.

She's hoping that he wins the bet.

To her, he is the most familiar-looking thing in this group of buyers...but what she doesn't know is that he would be one of her worst fates.

"T-ten credits!" The Zedice grins. "Any other offers?" He glances around the group. "Maybe ten and a half?"

I can hear the slight hope in his voice, which makes my disgust for him grow.

No one replies.

To them, the human looks like a dirty, weak, and strange thing. I do not think I have to worry about winning this bid.

"Twenty credits." My voice rings throughout the room, eliciting several gasps and everyone in the room turns to face me.

My cloak is still low, and I can see they are wondering just who I am. Nobody pays that much for a slave, especially one that will most likely be disposed of in a few days.

Keeping my head low, my body covered, I do not satisfy their curious gazes.

"T-twenty?!" The zedice almost forgets *he* is the one running the auction. That the money will be his and he will not be the one paying.

The moment this realization comes back to him, his grin increases.

"Twenty credits!" He announces. "And the creature belongs to the—"

"Twenty-five."

There is another collective gasp, as the buyers turn to look over at the velushan.

He's lifted himself off the wall, his gaze on me. His normally cool eyes are slowly turning red, the scales at the back of his neck no longer pulsing but turning red as well.

He is annoyed. Irritated. Well, he'll be downright outraged when I'm done.

I cannot help the slight smile that twists my lips, but I keep my gaze on the female. I'm here for, and I'm not leaving without her.

Her throat is moving, her eyes flicking between me and the velushan, and every time she glances my way, the fear in her eyes increases.

She is afraid of me…more than she is of the velushan.

For a moment, this makes a strange feeling go through me, before I realize that she cannot see me clearly. For all she knows, I am a shadowed version of death, unlike the velushan who has not concealed himself in any way.

There is suddenly silence around us and I can feel the eyes of every being on me., waiting for my reaction.

"T-twenty five," the zedice announces. "And the creature belongs to the—"

The human grips the cage, her eyes on me now too.

I don't know what she sees, but when I open my mouth and utter my next words, the surrounding collective gasp is all she needs to know that I am not leaving this room without her.

"Fifty credits."

8

Marion

It's clear that whoever this cloaked alien is, he just paid a shit ton of money for me.

I can see the interest in this mysterious alien rise in every other alien in this room. Even the one running the auction beside me is literally shivering with glee.

But I'm not so sure whether I should be happy or not.

Unlike the humanoid green alien standing against the wall, I have no idea what this cloaked alien is or what he looks like.

His voice is a deep baritone, one that vibrates the air in the room as he speaks.

It's the voice of someone that demands respect, if nothing else. But I can't go on that alone.

For all I know, he is the worst being that could buy me in this room.

Fifty credits, though. He doesn't even know if I can fulfill whatever work he'll want me to do.

I'm not completely versed on the exchange rate between New Earth dollars and galactic credits, but I can tell that he's just paid an extortionate amount.

A glance at the green alien I'd been hoping to buy me makes something sink in my chest.

His eyes have turned red and he is snarling a little, but apart from that, he eases back against the wall, his hateful gaze on the cloaked alien, and he says nothing.

I gulp, my eyes going back to the cloaked being as he takes a step forward.

I still cannot see underneath his cloak, and that sort of terrifies me.

"S-sold," the auctioneer announces quickly, as if afraid the buyer will withdraw his bid. There is no gavel for him to hit to finalize the sale, but I assume his words are enough.

My heart slams hard against my chest as I wait for the cage to open and my entire body aches as I try to rise so I can walk out. But instead of opening, the cage instead begins to rise. My eyes widen as I cling to one of the bars.

"What is the meaning of this?" the cloaked alien speaks.

"Your *cazia* must be *fuloy* at the back," the auctioneer says, "so we may continue the market here."

The cloaked alien says nothing, but I can almost feel the glare he shoots at the auctioneer.

The auctioneer stutters. "S-she will be ready for you when we are done here, I promise you."

"You take liberties with my time," the cloak-wearer says. "You will release her to me now or forget your payment."

The auctioneer's eyes widen a little and he stutters some excuses, throwing his hands up as if the request is something he cannot do.

"Either way," the cloaked alien says, "she is leaving with me…now."

There is a hush across the group of buyers, everyone looking at the auctioneer to see his next move.

He goes a little pale and flicks his stubby wrist toward my cage.

Without a pause, the cage begins to lower again.

My heart rate increases at this fact, and I cannot pull my gaze away from the cloaked alien below me.

He has the room transfixed. I do not think anyone even dares to breathe.

Just what is he…?

Who is he?

My cage lowers until it touches the floor, and the auctioneer turns to face me as he opens the door.

His gaze isn't on me, though. Instead, he is giving a sideways look at the cloaked alien who looms behind him.

I can barely see a bit of bronze skin when the cloaked alien tips his head a little.

It's enough for me to stare at him.

As soon as the doors are open, the auctioneer steps away, his wide eyes on the cloaked alien.

I expect the cloaked one to turn and leave, expecting me to follow, and I take a step out of the cage, my knees almost buckling, and the pain in my back scorching.

When muscular arms grasp me and I'm suddenly lifted off my feet, a yelp leaves my throat.

He's lifting me, bridal carry style, as the group of buyers parts to let us through.

Directly underneath the alien's cloak, I can finally see his face now and as the door opens and he steps out of the room, I am transfixed by rich golden eyes set in the most striking face I have ever seen in my life. The shadows his cloak creates only highlight his sharp jawline and sculpted features.

His eyes seem to glow in the shadows and once we are climbing the narrow stairs, they finally land on me.

Fuck.

He looks like a god.

I open my mouth to say something, to ask where he is taking me, but that's all my mouth does. It opens.

"Don't worry, you poor *repi goonu*. You are safe now," is all he says.

Safe?

Light hits us as he finishes the last stair, and we are once more above ground.

His gaze travels over me again, and even with his strange catlike eyes, I can see the rage building within him as his eyes travel over me.

I am dirty. Frail. Stinky.

"I-I can walk," I try to say, but he makes a sound in his throat that makes me hush before he heads through the smelly alleyway.

The sky is darker now and I do not know if it is because of the sun going down or the rising smoke filling the air. The amount of beings on the road, though, has not lessened.

As a matter of fact, it seems there are even more aliens on the road now than there were before.

The cloaked alien holds me close and heads in one direction. He doesn't stop until he reaches a building I don't have any idea the purpose of.

Lifting one foot, he kicks the door open and steps inside.

My neck aches as I try to turn my head so I can see around me. My whole body aches, but the fear and uncertainty surrounding my future puts a damper on my physical awareness.

The room is dark but by the silence, it's clear the place is mostly deserted. There are only a few metal pieces of furniture standing on the floor, and at the front, behind the counter, an alien turns to look at us.

"Visitors!" he says. His eyes are on stalks that rise above his oval head.

He rushes from behind the counter, and I notice he has four legs, but two arms.

"A room. The best you have," the cloaked alien says.

"Immediately!" the innkeeper says, slapping his arms together with glee.

I get the impression that the residents of this planet don't visit inns regularly.

He rushes around the corner, and I hear metal things clinking and falling as he searches for something.

"Make sure there is warm water," the cloaked alien begins talking again and I soon lose track of his words as he speaks quickly, dictating what I assume is a long list of requests. Trying to translate everything, it goes by too fast for me to catch.

This is the perfect moment for me to observe him though, and I tilt my head a little so I can look at him.

My heart skips a beat when my eyes meet his golden eyes.

He's been observing me the whole time, even while speaking to the innkeeper.

There's a look in his strange eyes that I cannot read. I do not know if he is angry or what he is thinking.

He is clearly observing me—has been clearly observing me—and that much sends a little shiver down my spine.

I gulp as I watch his lips move. Every now and then, the tips of what can only be fangs show. There is a light spattering of white hair on his face too—a silver beard.

This male is not human, but he could pass as one if he wore contacts maybe.

It is only when silence once more envelopes the room that I realize he's stopped talking and has begun to follow the innkeeper up a narrow staircase.

We can hardly fit.

Again, I try speaking to him.

"I don't know who you are, or what you intend to do with me, but I can walk," I say.

His gaze flicks over my face. "I am surprised you are even *pavrai*."

My brows furrow a little.

I do wish I had practiced Standard more often.

"Awake," the alien says, as if he notices my confusion.

"I am fine," I say.

He makes a sound in his throat just as we reach the landing and the innkeeper heads down the short corridor to the last door.

"Our most private quarters," he says, opening the door to reveal a small room.

A small bed is set in the middle of the room, barely big enough to hold two people. There is a raised metal object on one side, attached to the wall. The center is carved out in the shape of an egg and not far from it, there is another metal thing attached to the wall.

The toilet and bath I assume.

The only other thing in the room is a metal table and chair set on the other side of the wall.

"If there is anything else, please—" the innkeeper begins.

"Thank you. Your *greifin* is no longer needed," cloaked alien says, shifting me a little as he reaches underneath his cloak for something.

A golden coin is dropped into the innkeeper's hand. His eye stalks stiffen as his eyes widen.

"We are not to be disturbed," cloaked alien says.

The innkeeper's mouth falls open before he nods and hurries from the room, shutting the door quietly behind him.

And the silence envelopes the room immediately.

I am left alone with this strange male who has bought me.

I have no idea what his intentions are. No idea what he wants from me.

And this hits home when his gaze bores into mine and he speaks.

"Take your garments off."

9

Aqnar

I can feel every beat of the female's life organ as it thumps in her chest. It is slamming into her ribs erratically as she stares up at me.

She is calmer than I thought she would be. Possibly, she is still in shock.

I wish I could change that. Wish I could change what happened to her people, and if I encounter the Khuru who massacred her kind, I will make sure they pay.

Her mouth falls open as she stares up at me and I wonder if she understood my request.

Galactic Standard is the common language across the galaxy, but as her planet has only recently joined the Galactic Union, all its citizens may not yet know how to speak or understand it.

"Remove your garments," I repeat.

Her life organ speeds up.

She is so small. Much frailer than I thought her kind would be.

Though we have traded with the humans, such close contact with their females had been restricted.

That is why it had been so surprising they struck this deal, forcing their females on us in exchange for our technology. All we had wanted to trade for was a precious metal found on their planet. Gold, they call it. The color of the Atari eyes. A treasured metal for my kind. One the royal line wants to hoard.

We did not intend to trade for their females as well. It had been a bonus. Offered by the Earthkin government as a gesture of good relations.

As I set her down gently on the resting area, she winces and tries to hide it, her eyes going even wider as she looks at me.

I wonder how much of me she can see. Her eyes seem to get bigger and bigger, as if to draw in more light and it prompts me to remove the hood of my cloak.

I no longer have to hide.

A soft gasp leaves her lips as I release her and crouch before her.

Unlike what I thought, her eyes only grow bigger as they move over my face and my hair.

I wonder what she sees when she looks at me.

When I look at her, I see an unfortunate, small being who's been thrown a burden she does not deserve.

No female should have had to experience what she just went through. Especially not one so small and delicate.

For the first time since I took her into my arms, I take a good, proper look at her.

That's when I notice her arm. Or rather, the lack of it.

It's missing.

My gaze focuses on it, and she must notice because she shifts somewhat, turning slightly, a wince going through her, so I pull my gaze away.

Where is her prosthetic?

Maybe in the fight for her life, she somehow lost it?

No worries. Once she gets to Atar, I can fit her with a new, robotic one.

Her gaze is questioning as she watches me, her eyes never leaving my face.

"Who are you? What...do you want?" she whispers. Her voice is soft, melodious, despite the underlying uncertainty in her tone.

"I am Aqnar of the Atari."

"Atari?"

Hmm. She does not know of my kind.

It is possible her government did not disclose the deal they struck with us.

But they sent these females to us. Surely, she would have known she is being sent to be a mate for one of my kind.

"New Earth government must have mentioned us when you agreed to board that ship. You are to be a bride for the Atari."

She blinks at me, her brows going up. "I'm sorry, I don't...understand Galactic Standard very well. I'm translating your words to *bride*, but that can't be correct."

Activating the comms on my wrist, a small compartment opens, revealing a spare universal translator. I take up the small device and reach toward the female.

She jerks backward, her arm rising to block me.

"A translator," I say, showing her the chip on the tip of my finger before turning my head and pointing behind my ear where mine currently sits.

She stares at it before, slowly, she lowers her arm and I stick the disk to her temple, turning it on as soon as it is attached.

She winces as the frequency adjusts.

"Can you understand me?" I speak in Atari and a look of surprise lights up the female's eyes.

"Y-yes. I can." She brushes a finger over the translator.

"I am Aqnar," I repeat, my gaze moving over her face. "I am Atari. Me and my crew were sent to retrieve you and the other females who chose to be part of the bridal gift. When your ship was not where it was supposed to be, we searched for you and found...the massacre."

A myriad of emotions flick across her face.

"What?"

Can she still not understand? Perhaps the translator isn't—

"What bridal program?"

It is my turn to look confused.

"You are human, are you not?"

She jerks her chin slowly. "Yes, but...we were setting out on a luxury cruise. We're not part of a bridal program. I didn't sign up to be a bride. I think you are mistaken."

I am not.

I ease back on my haunches and release a breath as I watch the confusion grow in the female's eyes.

Fek.

This is more complicated than I thought it would be.

Rising, I turn away from the female as I move over to the washing tub and start the hot water.

She needs to wash the grime from her skin. It is only a reminder of what she went through. And she needs rest.

Accessing my communicator, I ping our main cruiser.

It takes a few moments before Qhenno answers my call.

"Qhenno," I say. "We have a problem."

"Aqnar! Have you found any of the females?"

"Yes." I glance behind me.

The female is watching me. A worried sort of confused look on her face.

"I have secured one. What about the others?"

"Others?" The female jumps to her feet and her knees buckle immediately.

I am at her side before she hits the ground.

I do not think she realizes just how injured she is.

She will need to be nursed back to health. There is no way I can take her back in my cruiser in this state.

Which means we will have to stay on Ockorius III for longer than I would prefer.

"Three others may have survived," I say, and hope flashes in her eyes.

I don't want to pull this hope away from her. We don't know if we will find them…or if we will find them alive.

I was lucky I found *her*.

"Da'red and Bhihan have both taken cruisers to the nearest stations in search of them. I am en route to another station as well," Qhenno says.

"It's possible they're alive," she whispers, and her eyes grow moist.

A sudden urge rises within me to lift a finger and wipe her sad waters away.

"Aqnar," Qhenno draws my attention. "My instruments tell me you are on Ockorius III." He pauses. "Be careful."

"As always," I reply.

10

Marion

Relief floods through me when I hear that Mona, Rissa, and Trudy may have survived. It makes my body sag on the big alien who is suddenly cradling me again.

Aqnar he said his name was, and if he's telling me the truth, then everything I thought I knew about this whole trip has been one big lie.

I fumble against him, trying to rise, but he does not let me.

Instead, he lifts me again and strides over to the swirling bathwater.

Without a word, he sets me gently into it.

It's warm and my body instantly melts.

Warm water is scarce on the lower levels of New Earth. Heating is expensive, so most do without.

The blood and dirt on my body instantly turn the water red and I swallow hard as I look down at it.

"Remove your garments," Aqnar says once more, and I stiffen a little.

I saw how he was looking at my nub. I'm surprised he didn't notice it before.

The last thing I want is him seeing *more* of my body.

"I…I don't want to get naked in front of you."

I shouldn't have looked up at him then because the look in his eyes sends a strange shiver down my body.

I don't know this male.

He is three times my size and could probably snap me in two if he wanted to.

The only thing I have to go on is the fact that he appeared out of nowhere, paid an exorbitant amount of money for me, and hasn't tried to harm me yet.

All I have to go on is what he has told me…and what I heard him say to his friend.

A slight smile twists his lips. "Do Earth humans still practice such archaic beliefs of modesty? I will turn around if it makes you feel better."

When I nod, his smile widens somewhat, transforming his features and flashing his fangs.

God, he is beautiful. Like a painting. The white, long hair that frames his head only highlights his bronze skin and eyes.

He turns as he's promised, and I'm left staring at his back.

As quickly as I can, I slip what's left of my maxi dress over my head.

I have to wash it and fix it somehow. I have no other clothes. Kicking off my slip-ons, I take them out of the water.

The bath is a swirling, filthy mess now and I stretch to find the stop that releases the liquid.

It takes me a few moments before I find it and the water begins to go down the drain. As soon as it's gone, I begin filling the bath once more.

All this time, Aqnar remains with his back turned.

"Will you be standing like that until I am finished?" I whisper.

"No. Just until you are comfortable enough for me to turn around."

His words make my brows furrow.

"Why do you want to turn around?"

"You are injured. You cannot tend to yourself."

My whole body aches and every movement sends shocks of pain through me, but that doesn't mean—

"Ready now?"

I don't get a chance to answer. Only enough time to spin so my back is toward him when he faces me once more.

The sudden growl that vibrates the air sends a shiver down my spine and I turn my neck so I can see him.

The look of sudden rage on his face has my eyes widening.

He grabs me by the shoulder, and it is only vaguely that I note his hold on me doesn't hurt even as he turns me farther away from him.

"*What is this*?!" he roars.

At first, I do not know what he means.

"They whipped you…" His words are said with a low growl. One that sends another shiver down my spine, even more than his roaring did.

Oh…the welts on my back. They burn every time the water brushes against them.

"**Who did this**?" the Atari growls.

I do not understand why my injury has elicited such a response from him. You would think I mean more to him than simply being a stranger he has found and decided to, hopefully, help.

"The, uh, the ones that killed…"

"**Fekking Khuru**," he growls. I can almost *feel* the rage emanating off him.

Silence envelopes us both.

I do not know how to respond.

It's been a long, long time since anyone has cared about my well-being. I've been on my own for as long as I can remember.

I feel I have to say something but a knock at the door saves me.

The Atari releases his gentle hold on my shoulder and stalks to the door, opening it enough that I see the innkeeper carrying a tray laden with several things.

His eyes widen as soon as he sees the Atari without his head cloaked, but as he opens his mouth to say something, the Atari grasps whatever he brought and closes the door without a word.

He sets the things down on the table before taking up two round objects and turns back toward me.

I'm staring.

It's only now that I look away.

When his fingers brush against my back, lightly skirting over the areas where my skin isn't broken, my body trembles and I jerk away from his hand.

It's been long since anyone has cared for me. Even longer since I have been *touched* in such a caring way.

He makes a sort of humming sound, similar to how a mother shushes a baby, and his voice surprises me.

"It will be okay, female. I will not let you hurt like this again." His voice is soft, filled with care. For such a big male, it's strange hearing him speak like that...and *to me*. I stiffen at his words and then he growls. "And I will break the neck of any being that tries."

His words catch me off guard so much that when he reaches for me again, pressing a soft sponge filled with warm water against my skin, I am so stunned I don't jerk away this time.

He makes that soft humming sound in his throat once more, and I stay still, unable to believe what is happening, as he washes the dirt from my wounds.

For a few minutes, that's all he does, moving so slowly and with such care, an outsider would think I am his lover and not someone he just met.

"W-why are you doing this?" I whisper.

I can't understand.

From the moment he made his presence known in that room filled with the buyers till now, all of his actions have confused me.

"You don't even know me..." I continue. "Why do you care? Why are you helping me?"

My back is still turned to him. He's still washing it, and frozen as I am, unable to move, I cannot see his face.

The movement of the sponge stops, and for a few moments, the Atari says nothing.

"I am helping you...because you need my help," he finally says.

I lick my lips.

Where I come from, help is never free.

"What do you want in return?"

He grunts and begins washing my back once more, careful not to disturb the deep welts.

"After you are safe on Atar, you owe me nothing, human."

I don't believe that. I may not know the details of everything. Hell, I might not even trust him completely and his reasons for assisting me, but he has saved my life and he is caring for me now when he doesn't need to.

It's more than I can say the very woman who birthed me would have done.

I have to repay him *somehow*.

But something he said finally dings in my head. "Safe on Atar? You're taking me to your planet?"

"I cannot return you to yours."

"But…"

"A trade was struck. An agreement signed," he says. "You are ours now. Your ties with your planet were severed the moment you boarded that ship."

But…

"That can't be. I…We…" I couldn't have been the only naïve, ignorant one. I don't think any of those women knew what we had been invited to. *What we signed up for.* That it had all been a ploy. That this "luxury cruise" was the government's way of getting rid of us. Their way of lessening the burden of the lower levels.

A spike of fear goes through me, one that has me feeling numb. My "cruise" wasn't the only one either. Another smaller one left New Earth the day before.

"Do not worry, female. You will not be mated if you do not wish. We are Atari. Our word is our bond."

I don't think he understands where my confusion is coming from, and as he dips the sponge in the water and continues to massage the grime from my back, I'm left looking into the water as it turns red around me.

This isn't real…is it?

Has my life been turned upside down in a single day, without me even realizing what I was walking into?

11

Marion

For the next few minutes, the Atari continues washing my back before he slowly begins to wash over my shoulders. When the sponge moves around to my neck, brushing lightly, I grab his wrist.

He stills, and a sound like a chuckle rumbles in his throat.

"Good grip," he says.

I clear my throat. "I can wash the rest of myself. You have helped me enough."

His hand stiffens under mine. "You will do no such thing."

But he releases me and steps away from the bath.

I think he is letting me do what I requested until I hear shuffling behind me.

Taking a chance, I glance back at him, only to do a double-take.

My mouth falls open as I watch the Atari's cloak fall to the floor.

It's impossible, but without the cloak, he looks even bigger.

Bulging muscles highlight his arms as he reaches behind him and unlocks his garments.

It's a dark leather sleeveless top with matching dark leather pants on the bottom to complement it.

He slips off his upper clothing easily, revealing a perfectly sculpted back.

I have never seen a more perfectly built male in my life. Not that I've had the luxury of seeing many males strip before me, but the few boyfriends I've had never came close to looking like *this*.

The Atari…Aqnar…is the type of male that only dwells on New Earth's upper levels, never venturing to Lower Earth unless for sketchy reasons.

I'm staring at him again, not realizing I am until his fingers trouble the latch that holds his pants at his waist, releasing the garment. It promptly falls to his feet.

A taut ass meets my gaze and a breath hitches in my throat when he suddenly turns around.

OhmyfuckingGod!

I spin around, water splashing around me and pain erupting across my back at my sudden movement.

"Whatareyoudoing? Whyareyounaked?"

"I cannot wash you properly unless I get into the water with you. I refuse to let you tend to yourself."

I hear him approaching and I skirt across the bath, putting distance between us.

He must be joking.

But the water moves, rising a little higher as he enters it, and I *feel* his presence behind me.

"I c-can wash myself."

"So you've said, yet you can hardly move without hissing in pain."

"I'm fine. Really. You don't have to do this."

"You're right, human. I don't have to do this. But I will."

I gulp. "Marion. My name is Marion."

He makes a "hmm"-like sound in his throat. "Marion," he repeats my name. "As soft a name as you are. Now, let me wash you. The sooner you hand me the sponge, the quicker we can get out of this bath. I do not enjoy soaking in the blood of slain women."

I gulp again, refusing to turn and face him. But he is so close, the skin all over my back prickles at his nearness.

"I can do it myself."

"So you have said."

Fuck, he's stubborn.

"This…this isn't appropriate. You're naked and…"

He makes a sound in his throat. "And…?"

"And…*I'm* naked. You could have left your clothes on."

He chuckles. It is a deep, low timbre that makes my skin shiver in a most delicious way.

"Ah, this is to do with your planet's modesty laws."

"They aren't *laws*. It's common decency," I bite back.

He chuckles again.

"How about you wash me some time when you are better, Marion? Would that make it even?"

The low timbre of his voice sends another shiver through me, and I have to shake my head to focus.

"No, it would not!" My cheeks warm. The thought of running my hands over the body I've just seen…My pulse quickens just thinking about it.

"Then let me wash you now. You are hurt. Let me take care of you."

I grip the sponge for dear life.

The thought of this gorgeous alien's hands roaming all over me, it elicits a response I did not expect. My heartbeat stutters, my clit throbs a little, and my entire body feels super aware of his lightest breath, his every movement.

It's a puzzling response, one I've never had so suddenly before.

"I…" I begin.

"Is it that you don't want me to take care of you?" he asks.

I gulp again.

Good question.

"I…I've never had anyone try before," I whisper, the words coming out of my mouth before my mind can stop me.

Why the fuck did I say that?

Aqnar doesn't move and in that beat of silence, I wish I could go back and erase the last few words I said.

"Well," he finally says, "I am here to take care of you now. Let me."

The battle is lost when his hand covers mine and the sponge slips from my fingers. Before I know it, a strong arm wraps around my waist and I am being pulled backward onto firm thighs.

My upper body rises above the water, enough that the top of my breasts hover at the surface.

"Tell me if you become uncomfortable. Tell me if it hurts," he says. "I will not harm you, Marion. Let me ease your pain."

12

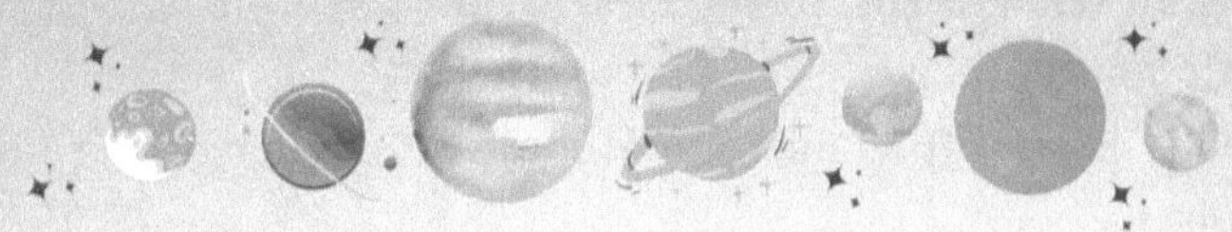

Aqnar

I try my best not to irritate Marion's wounds as I wash her.

Using the sponge infused with a mild antiseptic, I work my way over her shoulders as she sits rigidly in my lap.

Silence engulfs us, only the sound of the water breaks the tension as I dip the sponge and bring it to her body.

She doesn't move. It is as if she is afraid to, and I almost feel sorry for making her break her modesty laws. But she has not seen herself. She has not seen the discoloration all over her body. Large dark patches mark her skin, and even worse are the bloody wounds on her back.

I tilt my head to the side so I can look at her face and I spot another large wound on the side of her head.

I'm surprised she isn't unconscious.

When I've washed the parts of her body that are above the water, I rest the sponge on the bath's edge and grab the bar of soap. It too is antiseptic, and I create a lather before bringing my hands to her hair.

Marion inhales deeply but her gaze remains facing forward.

She opens her mouth though, words of protest on the tip of her tongue.

"It is easier if I do it," I murmur, and she visibly shudders at the sound of my voice.

I take my time, letting my fingers run through her hair, and with the silence growing between us once more, it is not lost on me that the position we are in is a very…intimate one.

I didn't have to wash her. She was right about that. I do not know what gods, or what devils, pushed me to do so.

But I do not regret it.

Her body is so soft against mine…her soft inhales taking my mind to other places…

It has been a long time since I have cared enough about any female to spend intimate time around them…

But I will not force myself on Marion. I would never do such a thing.

And in her state…

Still, that doesn't stop my body from responding when she shifts on my lap.

My cock throbs without my input.

"Are you uncomfortable?" I ask as I rinse her hair.

Marion's little pink tongue wets her lips, and she takes that moment to dip her hand in the water, swirling her fingers around in it.

As the grime disappears in the water, she looks even softer and more delicate than I first thought.

Small, pert pink lips fit neatly underneath her button nose. And those eyes of hers look big on her face. Highlighted by her dark hair, she is a beauty to behold.

I find myself pausing as I stare at her.

"Are you finished?"

Her question catches me off guard. "Finished with what?"

"Washing me." She glances sideways but does not focus on me directly. "I can do the rest."

Right.

I must wash the rest of her.

My gaze falls to the mounds on her chest. They are lifted high, buoyant because of the water. They look even softer than the rest of her body.

My cock takes this most inopportune moment to throb again, and Marion grips the side of the bath.

She felt it.

"Maybe it is best—" I begin.

"That I do the rest myself?"

A chuckle rises in my throat at how quickly she finishes the sentence.

"Aye."

She slides off my lap before I can help her, a wince going through her as she moves to the other side of the tub.

This time, she turns to face me, her arm covering the mounds on her chest.

"Thank you," she says.

I blink at her. Her gratitude catches me off guard.

"My pleasure," I reply.

Bad choice of words.

Her cheeks grow warm and when I rise before her, her eyes become large pools as they settle on my crotch.

But she does not look away. She keeps her gaze locked, her mouth falling open, as she watches me leave the bath.

I don't need to look at where her gaze is pointed. I already know my cock is hard and standing upright.

But unlike this little female and her modesty laws, the Atari have no such rules.

I do not mind showing her my nakedness.

When I turn my back, reaching for my garments, her soft voice breaks the silence.

"Are you…Are you being truthful when you say you want nothing from me?"

The insinuation is clear and the growl that leaves my throat is immediate as I spin to face her.

There's still that redness in her cheeks as she stares back at me, gripping her mounds and looking everything like the helpless being that she is.

My nostrils flare, my eyes burning with growing rage. The worst thing one can do is insult an Atari in such a way. Ignoring all aspects of modesty, I grip my cock in my palm.

"Don't let this natural response fool you, human. I would never force a mating on you." Her cheeks grow even redder and I pause, my anger dissipating at her obvious embarrassment. She didn't mean to upset me. "Unless that is what you want…"

I'm not surprised when she stutters, the water splashing as she forgets she's protecting her modesty and hits the water with her arm. "A-Absolutely not."

I grunt, a smile coming to my lips. "Thought so."

13

Marion

I'm beginning to believe that though this alien has rescued me, he is a stubborn, insufferable, brute.

I frown at him as he dons his leather clothing, looking every bit like some medieval conqueror. All he needs is a battle axe and a trusty steed.

"I will leave you to wash your…intimate parts, since I am sure you will crawl out of your skin if I try to."

I stutter to find a quick response. The thought of his hands touching me, gripping my breasts, running the sponge across my pussy…it's so vivid, it has me momentarily speechless.

"When I come back, I will apply this healing ointment to your wounds." He takes up a metal tin from the tray the innkeeper had brought. "And bind them." He brushes the binding that's there too, ignoring the fact I'm blushing redder than the latest rouge the higher-ups use for blush nowadays.

"W-where are you going?" I don't know why I ask.

What does this man—Atari—owe me? Nothing. Yet, in the space of this short time, I owe him everything.

He doesn't answer me and when he turns to face me, those gorgeous golden eyes narrow on me.

"Planning on running away?" he asks.

I shake my head. "Of course not."

"Good." He tightens his trousers and pulls his cloak over his frame. "Because what's out there is worse than what you think I am."

My mouth falls open then closes. I cannot argue. I'd just insinuated that he wanted to use me in his bed. But after seeing his cock (and God knows, it's not just any sort of cock…it's a *godly* cock…and it was hard…and throbbing!), it's the first thing that came to my mind.

Back on New Earth, the lower levels are infested with males who want to use females like me for a fun time. Women with "defective genetic material" are seen as nothing more than that. Defective. Not to mention that the majority of humans no longer form life bonds. Marriage died eons ago. Apart from fun and for casual relationships, people no longer have sex for continuation of the species or to form families.

That's why I should have run from that ship the moment I entered it and realized every female there was like me. The fact I believed the government would do something so nice for someone like *me*…a defective being.

I'm barred from so many things '*normal*' humans have access to, even those from the lower levels. Everyone needs a license to bear young, and my eggs will never be harvested, simply because my genes aren't desirable. I am forbidden from becoming a mother. I am forbidden from forming a life bond. I am forbidden from tainting the gene pool in any way.

It's something one accepts. It's normal in New Earth society.

I close my eyes for a few moments, taking a deep breath as I shake my head.

I was so stupid.

Luxury cruise, my ass. I wanted it so badly…I didn't even notice the red flags even though they were right in my face, blowing in the wind.

When I glance up, Aqnar is watching me closely and the intensity of his gaze holds me arrested.

"I will not leave you here, Marion, if that is what you're thinking."

I allow a ghost of a smile to cross my face. He must have misunderstood the shadows that crossed my eyes as sadness or anxiety about him leaving me.

"I know you won't," I say. And…it's the truth. He's gone through so much trouble already, I believe he won't leave me here. I am indebted to him, and despite what he's said so far, I'm sure I will have to repay that debt somehow.

Things are never free. There is always a cost.

Aqnar stares at me before his gaze falls to my lips and then to my breasts, buoyant in the water.

I don't know why I don't try to cover myself.

"How do you know?" he asks, his gaze slowly moving back up to my eyes.

I shrug. *Because reality is a bitch and I know my thoughts are right.* That's what I want to say, but instead I go with, "I trust you."

Aqnar nods, as if my trust in him is easy to believe. And I guess it is. He has been nothing but gallant since the moment I met him.

He settles the hood of the cloak over his head, disguising his features once more, before he turns toward the door.

"Remain in the water till I return. I will not be gone for long."

I nod and with that, he heads toward the door.

14

Marion

I finish washing myself as best as I can. It's hard, and I realize that Aqnar was right about my wounds.

There are a lot more than I first thought I had.

Most of my body aches, but I manage to clean myself completely, release the water, and rinse myself off one more time before climbing awkwardly from the tub.

There's a folded cloth that's on the tray the innkeeper brought in, just large enough to act as a towel, and with nothing else to use, I pull it across my body to dry myself. It's coarse and scratchy but I work diligently, getting all the water off.

The place is so quiet, that every little breath I take sounds like a huge sigh, but I welcome the quiet.

Knowing what outside on the streets is like, it's surprising no sound filters in. I cannot even hear the innkeeper downstairs.

Grabbing the ointment and the gauze, I settle on the bed and begin to tend to my wounds.

I know Aqnar said he would bind them for me, but I'm not an

invalid. I'm capable of tending to myself, despite my disability, and besides, he's done enough for me.

As soon as I get better, I have to focus on repaying him for his kindness and figuring out a way to return to my miserable life on New Earth.

Reaching across my back to get the ointment into my wounds would be a feat for even a person with two arms, but I somehow make do. I know I miss a lot of spots, so I unroll the long strip of bandage and cake some of the ointment along it as well. Holding one end between my teeth, I pull to create some tension and grip the other end with my hand.

Bringing the gauze around myself for several revolutions, I wrap it tight until I'm sure I've covered every inch of broken skin on my back. Then I tuck the ends in.

The whole process takes a while and I collapse on the bed in a huff, my energy spent. Crawling into the middle, my chest heaves as I stare at the gray metal wall before me.

The silence envelopes me and I reach for the damp towel, covering myself before I pull my legs up to my chest.

I don't expect it, but that's when the tears finally come.

They run down my cheeks, soaking the bedding beneath me.

The horror of what happened on that ship begins to replay in my mind, and I grip my legs tighter to myself.

If what Aqnar says is right, then I know returning to New Earth isn't really an option—regardless of what I want to believe, and regardless that it's the only home I know.

The government will never accept me back. They would never risk the news of what they've done being disclosed.

I grip myself tighter.

I'm alone.

The moment I accepted that e-vite for that cruise, I sealed my fate.

What am I going to do now?

Aqnar

It's eerily quiet as I open the door to the quarters. The room is dark, but I have no problem seeing that the bath is empty.

A low curse hisses from my lips.

I've been gone for much longer than I intended.

Finding clothes that can fit a small human in a place like this turned out to be much harder than I anticipated. In this section of Ockorius III, clothing shops aren't really a thing. Those that come here usually keep the clothes on their backs and wear nothing else until they leave.

I found something, though, and even went back to my shuttle to grab a second cloak.

So yes, I've been gone for some time, but I had trusted the female when she'd said she wouldn't leave.

However, the bath is empty, the water drained, and there is no light in the room.

It is not until I step in and close the door that I see the small frame curled up in the middle of the sleeping area.

I stop in my tracks, staring at her.

The scent of ointment fills the room, and it's clear she tended to herself while I was gone. Some guilt fills me at that realization. She shouldn't have had to tend to herself in her state.

As I set the garments down on the table, the sound of my arrival does not rouse her.

She is fast asleep, and I drift closer to her sleeping form.

This human, Marion…she is so small.

I can't help the ache that goes through me as I look down at her. To know the pain she's just experienced.

For her own people to abandon her…it is unthinkable.

My gaze moves over her face. Now clean, her straight dark hair lies softly against her pale skin, creating a contrast that's striking.

It is not just her eyes that are beautiful to look at.

She is beautiful as well.

A shiver goes through her, and she lets out a soft whimper.

She's only draped a damp piece of cloth over herself to ward off the cold, and with the night coming in, these metal walls will do nothing to retain warmth.

Slipping off my cloak, I take the damp piece of cloth away.

She's curled up into a ball, her knees against her chest, making her appear even smaller and more vulnerable than before, and as soon as the damp cloth is removed, another shiver goes through her.

My gaze slips down her nakedness before I can stop myself.

Bruises dot her entire body and once again, I am angered by the actions of the Khuru.

Growling underneath my breath, I move my coat to cover her naked form. It will at least provide some warmth. Easing back, I gaze down at her once more.

I itch to stretch forward and run a finger down her cheek. My hand is already outstretched when I stop myself.

She already thinks I'm prone to take advantage of her. There's no need to make that feeling worse.

I'm about to move away when a whimper leaves her lips, her chest heaving as she cries out.

"N-no! What are you doing?!"

Jerking back, at first, I think she is talking to me, but when her eyes remain closed, her body still shuddering, I realize she isn't awake.

This is a sleep terror.

She is reliving the horror of what happened in her dreams.

"No!" She screams again, thrashing so hard, she throws my cloak off her.

I do the only thing I can think of doing.

Kicking off my boots, I climb onto the bedding with her.

It's only large enough to hold one person and I end up pulling her right into my arms and flush against me.

"Hush now, little one," I murmur into her hair. "You are safe."

Her jerking calms down but she whimpers again, spinning so she is facing me as she buries her face into my chest.

The movement causes an unexpected reaction.

A need to protect this female with everything I have surges within me, and I stare down at her before I wrap my arms around her and pull her even closer.

She whimpers again as I soothe her, and soon she is still once more, the only thing making her body heave being her soft breaths as she breathes against me.

Burying my face into her hair, I grip the nape of her neck and close my eyes, allowing myself this one moment to comfort her as I would my mate, if I had one.

"I'm here, Marion," I whisper.

When we left Atar to tow a ship full of females, I never thought I'd become attached to one. She's been through so much…

Her resilience in contrast to her softness and fragility…it impresses me…

If I could take her pain, I would, but all I can do is pull her closer.

In this short time of being in her presence, I can already tell that she is a sweet soul. And, right at this moment, I know if anyone tries to harm her, I will kill them with my bare hands.

15

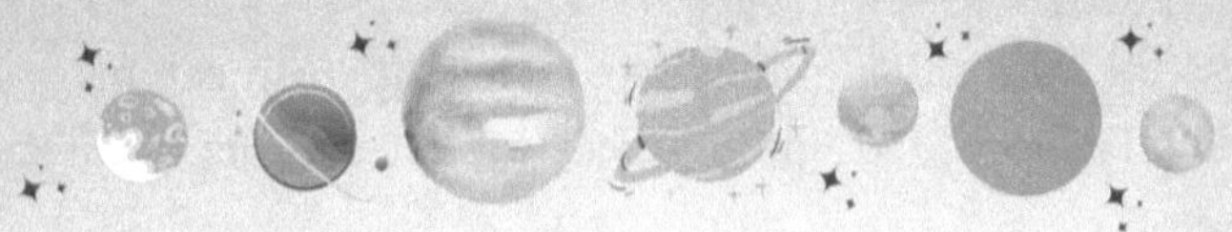

Marion

I don't know how long I've been asleep, only that when I wake, it feels like a lot of time has passed.

It's surprisingly warm and comfortable and a unique scent wafts into my nose.

Musk and spice.

Male.

I inhale deeply, forgetting for a moment the events of the past day, and then it all comes flooding back like a tidal wave.

My eyes fly open to see a bare bronze chest—the source of the musk and spice—and the shock causes me to jerk backward.

But I go nowhere. Strong arms tighten around me, pulling me back against the hard chest.

I lie there, stunned.

"Aqnar?"

"Yes, little female?"

"What—How did I end up here?" I remember falling asleep, but not in his arms. I don't even remember him returning last night.

"I rescued you from the Zedice's market, remember?" His voice is drowsy, gravelly with sleep, and utterly sexy in the way he drawls.

I find my heartbeat quickening for a whole other reason than our proximity.

Making an effort to move away once more doesn't produce any results.

"Stay," he growls.

I clear my throat. "Surely you'll be more comfortable *without* me taking up space on the bed?"

"Nonsense," he says, and when I look up to meet his half-open eyes, a devilish lopsided smile graces his face. "This is the best I've slept in ages."

There is a rumble in his chest as he adjusts himself, pulling me even closer.

"I didn't take all my garments off. Don't worry. I know you would probably try to run away if you awakened with my cock pressing into your naked belly."

His words make me go still.

Oh fuck. That's right. *I'm naked!*

I glance over at the tub.

In my tiredness yesterday, I never got to wash what's left of my maxi dress.

Shit.

In my obvious mortification, Aqnar chuckles, causing me to frown up at him.

"What's so funny?"

"I was right. You wish to escape."

I slap my hand against his chest and that makes him chuckle even more.

"What? You think you're so hot I can't resist you or something? Or that I've never seen a cock before? Or that I'm afraid of cocks?!"

He shrugs, causing me to move against him, but doesn't answer. If it wasn't for the bandage I wrapped all around my chest, my bare nipples would be rubbing all over his torso.

"Let me make one thing clear. You rescued me yesterday, but I'm not some damsel in distress. I'm also not some virginal idiot who has never seen a man before. I wouldn't flinch even if your cock was in my face."

The moment his eyes pop open is the moment I realize what I just said.

My cheeks grow warm.

"You wouldn't, would you? We can always test that theory…" Aqnar murmurs.

I let out an exasperated grunt and he chuckles again, one hand absently moving to rub my back in languid strokes.

"Just relax," he murmurs. "I will not take advantage of you. This is my oath. One you can trust. I simply enjoy the feel of your body next to mine…and I think you enjoy mine as well."

I roll my eyes but don't answer and he chuckles again.

"Glad you find this so amusing," I murmur.

"It distracts from the situation," he replies before going silent.

He's right. The situation that brought us to this moment has to be one of the worst things that could ever happen in anyone's life.

I remain silent too, allowing the minutes to tick by between us as this large male strokes my back like I'm his lover.

I dare to let myself relax. To let his touch soothe me.

The fact he does it as if we've known each other for years is… strange to me but oddly *comforting*. Fewer formalities, fewer barriers… it's…uncomplicated.

"You feel no pain when I touch you here?" His voice is so low now, it makes his chest vibrate.

"On my back?" I pause, my brows furrowing. "Surprisingly…no."

"Good," he murmurs. "The ointment has a numbing effect. I am pleased it is working."

I never told him thanks, and I murmur it now. "You've done a lot for me. I…I appreciate it. I appreciate everything. If you never found me in that auction room…"

He makes a low comforting sound that he's done before—a deep rumbling purr that makes my muscles relax.

"But I *did* find you and you are safe now."

I nod, a lump forming in my throat. His generosity…his kindness… it's almost too much to understand.

"What will happen to the little creature that no-one bought?"

"The newot?" he asks.

"I'm not sure of the species name. He was the first to be auctioned…and no one bought him." Memory of his cries make me shudder and Aqnar pulls me closer.

"Newots bond to one host family and can never bond to another. They become its everything. He was doomed the moment they abandoned him."

I tilt my head to look up at him. "That's…horrible. Who could ever abandon something that needs them so badly?" Resting my forehead back on his chest, I try to quell the pain hearing about the creature's fate brings.

"I was abandoned once," I murmur, not able to stop the words before they tumble from my lips. "It is not something I'd wish on another creature. If I could have helped him, I would have."

"Even while knowing he would never be truly happy? Never be truly loyal to you?"

I nod, and Aqnar doesn't reply.

Instead, his hand moves to the nub of my short arm, and the sudden touch on that spot causes me to jerk away from him.

"Your arm…" he whispers, and I squeeze my eyes shut for a moment.

I was wondering when he would ask about it.

But his question is not about how I lost it, or whether I was born with it like that. He says something completely different.

"Tuck it here, underneath mine. You will be warmer."

I am stunned in silence as he moves my body so my short arm is tucked inward, pressed against him. He's not…

He's not grossed out by it?

I blink into his chest, not understanding. Not daring to consider it either.

"Did you lose your prosthetic during the massacre?"

"Prosthetic?" I repeat, his words taking me out of my daze.

"Yes. I…" He pauses as if searching for the right words. "I saw the security footage of your ship. Saw you helping the other females. Surely, you lost it then."

I shake my head, still in a daze that he's accepted the fact I'm different so easily. "I...I've never had one."

He stiffens and when I glance up, he is frowning.

"Your world leaders did not provide you with one?"

"Ha!"

He blinks down at me, his eyebrows shooting upward, and I sober up when I realize he's serious.

He's...really not joking. He actually thinks the government would have provided something I needed. It says a lot about the world he comes from, Atar.

"If I wanted a prosthetic, I'd have to get the money for it on my own, and the ones on Lower Earth aren't worth the money you pay for them. Finding one that isn't riddled with problems would be like finding a thousand credits. I learned to manage without one."

"Doesn't that make your life...difficult?"

I shrug. "I serve drinks in a bar for a living, and I manage fine. I'm used to the arm not being there. At this point in my life, suddenly having two arms might actually be hard to adjust to."

His hand lands on my nub and I resist the urge to jerk away from his touch. I have to make a conscious effort not to pull myself away. I've always been self-conscious of people touching me there, and now, especially him.

Aqnar is...*perfect*. Him touching the most vulnerable part of me makes me feel...*exposed*.

But his touch isn't exploratory or curious. He simply rubs my nub like he was rubbing my back.

"Your skin," he whispers, "is so soft."

His gaze moves over me, and I find I cannot look away from him.

No man on Earth has ever looked at me like that before.

I can't decide if that's a good or a bad thing. So far, Aqnar has been nothing but a gentleman. I don't want to get used to it. There's a lot of shit out there. Shit I will have to inevitably return to.

"As soon as we land on Atar, I will have a prosthetic especially made for you, if you wish," he concludes.

I blink at him. "You were serious," I whisper.

"Serious about what?" As he continues rubbing my arm, his eyes go back to that drowsy state they were in when I woke up.

"About taking me back to your planet."

"That is where you now belong." His eyes open. "Unless there is somewhere else you want to be." His gaze falls to my lips. "Or someone you want to be with?"

I watch as Aqnar's gaze moves over my lips before dragging back to my eyes almost unwillingly.

I shiver a little and I am not cold.

I'm not imagining this, am I?

This is incredibly sensual.

Aqnar is making my heart beat unnaturally. Every neuron in my body is aware of his slightest touch and his every breath. Try as I might to ignore it, I can't.

Are all Atari like this?

It will take some getting used to.

"Do you?" The alien asks, his voice taking on a note of something I'm almost afraid to decipher. Anticipation? Envy?

"Do I what?" I whisper.

I'm in this alien's arms, snuggled against his chest, and he's wrapped around me like I'm some precious thing in this universe that he's just found.

Yesterday, I was in a cage.

Surely, I'm dreaming.

"Do you have someone you must return to?" He pauses, his golden eyes growing intense. "Did your leaders rip you away from your mate?" His voice deepens. "From young?"

I blink a thousand times. He's asking if I have a male friend and children. A *family*.

I scoff a little, possibly to hide my surprise and the awkwardness that his question causes to rise within me.

"People like me don't have those things," I whisper finally.

Aqnar stops rubbing my nub to press a finger underneath my chin, forcing me to look up at him.

"People like you? Explain this."

I sigh but meet his gaze. "As you've noticed, I'm not whole." I choke out those horrible words like they taste rotten. "Females and males like me don't get a chance to breed. I have no children to go back to. No partner. If I was deserving—"

His finger forces my chin up once more and I realize my head had tilted downward while I spoke. The absolute fire in his eyes almost scorches me.

"*Deserving*?" He growls. "I have fought many battles on Atar. I have seen death and massacre. Blood and gore. I have seen my brothers cut down before me and I have seen worlds torn apart."

I don't know why, but his words make me tremble and everything that happened on that ship comes flooding back.

"What I saw you do on that ship, Marion, in the midst of the chaos all around you…what you did is worthy of the highest medals for bravery and strength. And what you have revealed to me about yourself…you are selfless, caring, honorable…"

Aqnar looks straight into my eyes, and I know he believes what he's saying to me, wholeheartedly.

"Deserving?" He growls again. "Any male would be lucky to be deserving of you."

I am struck by his words, my eyes searching his for the moment he will break his intense gaze and laugh in my face, calling me a sucker for even wanting to believe him.

Instead, his face dips, coming closer, and when his lips pause before mine, the world stands still.

There is a moment that passes between us, one where I'm caught in a world that shouldn't exist, and as my breath brushes against his lips, Aqnar's head dips completely. His lips brush against mine in a kiss that shatters my perception of the world around me.

16

Aqnar

Marion's lips are like the sweetest, most intoxicating mead, and as soon as our lips touch, I find myself groaning and pulling her into me.

She whimpers, a soft sound that sends a shockwave through me, hardening my cock in my trou and causing the swelling head to rise and press against her.

It was not my intention for any of this to happen. I did not intend to get close to this female in this way.

But ever since I held her in my arms and carried her from the cage in that dreadful room, I realize I have been drawn to being close to her.

The bath…

Comforting her in her sleep…

I want to touch her always. My fingers itch to be pressed against her skin.

"Marion," I groan her name as her lips open to mine, tracing her soft flesh with my tongue.

I want this female.

I should have known from the moment my eyes caught hers in that security feed. The sudden protective urge that surged through me then was enough proof.

Her arm rises to my neck, clasping me softly there as she tilts her head and her eyes flutter closed.

Her tongue flicks against mine, causing my cock to harden even more, and when her fingers brush against the nape of my neck a deep growl rumbles through me.

My cock throbs immediately, straining painfully against my trou, and I can feel the preseed bursting at my tip.

How did she know the back of the neck is an Atari's weakest spot, not only in battle but in mating as well?

That touch just sent my primal urges into overdrive and it takes every ounce of restraint for me to grab her hand and push her *away* from me.

Marion's eyes fly open, searching mine, hurt spreading through her pupils.

"I—" I begin, but controlling the urge to pin her down and push my cock between her folds is almost taking all of my will.

*I want to mark her. To take her pain. Make her safe. Make her **mine**. With me no harm will come to this beautiful being ever again.* My eyes widen. *Fek. **I want to mark this female.** I want her to carry my bite.*

Marion pulls her hand away, her throat moving as she shuffles away from me.

I let her go. Realization that the base of my cock is throbbing at just the taste of her lips, is slowly sending me into shock.

Atari only mark their true mates. It's an instant connection, one that blooms as soon as the two meet and they scent or touch each other. But with the number of mateable females dwindling over the last few centuries, the number of unmated males has grown.

It is a dream for many…and it was a dream for me too. Until now.

My life organ hammers against my chest, making it hard to breathe, as I stare at the female before me in shock.

I had not known. If I had…

That instant connection between Atari…it was missing when I met Marion. All my life I have heard stories from mated men, of the immediate urge to bed and bite their mates. Of the undeniable urge to rut.

But Marion is human. That urge was missing when I first met her. First touched her.

Qef me.

My mate is human.

The difference in our species must be the reason for the delay in my natural urges. And as I stare at her, how small she is, delicate, frail, I know that was probably for the best. I would have slaughtered everyone in that room at just the sight of her in that cage.

Just thinking about it now, the skin at my spine tingles and tightens even though there is no threat here. There is that impulse and the distinct desire to pin this little female beneath me and fill her pussy with my cock, locking us together and keeping my spend deep inside her until her belly swells with my young.

I…

I have a mate. And she's right before me.

Never did I imagine this day would begin like this. But, caught up in my own revelation, the seconds that pass have Marion moving even farther away from me.

The sleeping area is small, but the little space she has put between us suddenly feels like a million leagues. A pain develops within my chest.

I am reluctant to let her go, but if I touch her now, I know I might scare her. And…I do not want to take her like this. Not when she reeks of fear and woe. She is human. She does not understand Atari biology or customs. *And she is mine.* I know it as well as I know I exist. That I am alive and that I am Aqnar. I will not harm her in any way.

When I do take her, I want it to be slow. I want to enjoy every inch of her, and I want her to enjoy every inch of me.

She clears her throat and rises, pulling the cloak around herself, hiding her luscious soft body from me as she sits at the edge of the sleeping area, her back turned to me.

"That's clothes, right? For me?" She gestures to the garments I brought but doesn't wait for my answer. "I should get dressed."

She doesn't meet my gaze and the sudden change in her dissipates the tightening in my spine. I have done something wrong. I have hurt her.

"Marion," I begin. "I—"

How do I let her know that in the space of this short time, I have been drawn to her like I have been drawn to no other? That the thought of her being *mine* is already beginning to consume me?

Humans do not fall so easily. Our research into their species proved this. They do not even have pair bonds anymore, much less mate bonds. Their entry into our society was supposed to be a slow, smooth process. The human females were supposed to go through prepared courses, learning about our world, traditions, way of life before being allowed among the general population. And for the sole reason that as females, they would surely get a lot of attention from unmated males. Mate bonds could suddenly occur.

Like now.

Atari males can become possessive when they find their mates, and Earthkin are not used to that. Marion will not understand if I told her what I want to do to her, even if I tried to explain.

I need time…

Time to show her that my life changed the moment I saw her on that security feed.

But this is not the place to do this…or the situation.

She's already pulling the garments over herself by the time I rise, her back still to me.

"I'll be ready in a few minutes," she says. "Then we can leave. You don't have to take me to your planet." She pauses. "And if I can't return to Earth, I'm sure there's somewhere else you can leave me. A refugee station or something. I can find my way. Find a job. Support myself. And pay you back too." She pauses again. "I thank you for all that you've done for me. I won't request anything else from you."

A growl rumbles through me at her words. They anger me…and sadden me at the same time.

She doesn't understand, but I cannot explain. A part of me is…*hesitant* to.

I cannot simply tell her I pushed her away because I was on the brink of spreading her legs and sliding *something* deep into her folds.

My cock…*or my tongue*. I wonder what she tastes like.

The thought makes me stifle a needy whimper.

She cannot know this. It would scare her.

"You're not going anywhere." The words come out a bit more gruffly than I intend, and she spins to look at me, a frown marring her brow.

"Excuse me?"

"You must eat," I say, the deepness in my voice causing me to clear my throat so I don't sound like I am angry toward her. "You must eat and rest. Staying on this gods-forsaken planet for more than a few days is a bad idea, but I will not leave until you are well enough to do so. My cruiser isn't meant for long-distance travel. It will not be a comfortable journey."

There is a hardness in her eyes that wasn't there before. One I am pained to see. She is angry at me.

"Then we should leave now," she says. Again, she underestimates her injuries.

"You are ill. If something should happen to you while on my cruiser..."

"I'll take the risk." That hardness doesn't leave her gaze. "I don't like being in this place."

Neither do I.

I want her in my quarters, in my home, her legs open on my bed.

"I don't like keeping you away from what you should be doing either." She releases a breath, her shoulders sagging. It is only then that I realize she's been keeping herself rigid this whole time. "I feel fine. I slept well last night. I'm not as weak or tired as I was yesterday, and my wounds aren't hurting either." She grabs the cloak I brought her and begins pulling it over her frame. It will dwarf her. It's meant to fit a full-grown Atari male, and when it settles over her, the urge to protect her surges within me.

"I'll accept the food," she says, "but we should go."

I want to object, but something tells me that if I don't give her this, whatever negative feelings I have caused by pushing her away will only grow stronger.

"Remain here," I say. "I will get the sustenance and when I return, we will head to my cruiser and leave this place." And I will explain this as simply as I can: she is mine and I am going to take care of her.

She nods. "For New Earth?"

A beat of silence passes between us.

"For somewhere else," I reply. I cannot take her back to her planet…but I also cannot take her to Atar if she doesn't want to come with me. I do not want her to despise me.

Little does she know though. If her intent is to pull away from me, requesting that I leave her on some rock won't work.

If she doesn't want to go to Atar, then I will go where she wishes, and I will remain there with her. Now that I have found the thing most precious to all Atari, I am never letting her go.

17

Marion

Silence engulfs the room the moment Aqnar leaves, and I remain on my feet, pacing back and forth.

He pushed me away.

The moment I let my guard fall, to hope that I could be more than what I present physically, he shot me down.

I don't know why I thought he was different.

Males on New Earth often can't overlook the fact I have a disability. Why would an alien that looks like he's been carved on Mount Olympus want anything to do with me?

Rolling my eyes, I wrap my arm across my chest and my pacing picks up.

I was stupid.

It's not like I haven't been through this before. Rejection is a familiar emotion. Taking a deep breath, I try to calm the illogical hurt that I feel deep in my heart, but the memory of Aqnar's lips has my fingers rising to brush my own.

That simple touch, the feel of his tongue, sent shockwaves through me.

I'm sure he felt it, too. I felt his cock harden against my belly, felt my pussy clench as he growled my name. Oh my God, I'm so desperate I would have let him fuck me right there and then.

I squeeze my eyes tight.

So stupid.

I've never considered myself as someone who falls easily, but the gods in the heavens know, *I would have let Aqnar fuck me.*

My chest rises and falls as I release a huge breath.

What the hell is wrong with me? The feeling is so intense. Even now, if he came back and tried to kiss me again, I would let him.

Isn't that the definition of insanity?

But...my body wants what my mind says is illogical.

He's been nothing but nice, nothing but gentlemanly, if a little forward. He came to rescue me, little old me, when he didn't have to. My own people abandoned me and sold me without me knowing, yet he, a *stranger*, has shown me nothing but care and tenderness since the first moment he touched me.

Oh my God.

I groan and bury my face in my palm as I pace, trying to erase the feeling of rejection that's swimming around me ever since he pushed me away. I shouldn't feel bad. *I have no reason to.* It was just a kiss... I'm not some inexperienced teenager that's never been turned down before. And what if he has a wife back home? A family.

God, Marion. Get a hold of yourself!

Minutes turn into what feels like at least an hour, and the whole time, I wear down the flooring in the room with my pacing.

"Maybe it's his kindness. Maybe that's what makes me drawn to him like he's got a magnet in his pants." I talk to the metal walls as if they can hear me. "And maybe I'm just deprived of goodwill. So much so that the first person who has shown me an ounce of kindness has touched that lonely, *needy* part of me."

I bite my fingers as I turn and continue pacing. Those words came from somewhere deep, and I'm contemplating them when the door handle to the room turns.

My heart skips a beat and I stop in my tracks.

He's back.

But something, I don't know what, makes the hairs at the back of my neck rise.

Maybe it's the way the door opens…slowly…too slowly…as if the person opening it isn't sure just what they will find inside.

Maybe that's what makes me take a step back, my eyes wide as the door finally opens fully, and the person standing there isn't Aqnar at all.

My eyes meet the cold, green ones of the murderer that started this mess in the first place. They are eyes I never thought I would see again, and the terror they incited the first time I saw them comes flooding right back.

Aqnar

I grip the metal box with the sustenance I procured. I filled it to the brim with different items, yet I wish I could have gotten Marion more. And *better*.

The options on Ockorius III leave much to be desired and what the innkeeper had in stock was not suitable. A food vendor had been my next best bet.

Dry, tasteless buns and various forms of broth I'm sure Marion will not ingest fill the box. If not for several galactic credits, I wouldn't have squeezed the stale fruit out of the vendor either.

I do not know what they taste like, but I hope she likes them.

It gives me some hope that I can lift her mood and explain why I pulled away from her, now that my cock isn't trying to force itself out of my garments and my fangs aren't dripping with the need to bite her. My mind is clear.

My thoughts are only drawn away from her when I feel a slight tug on my coat. I glance down at the newot there. Although fully grown, he is the size of a child, his head barely reaching my knee.

Regardless that it had taken more time away from Marion, I had returned to the Zedice's auction room. Seeing my face once more had sent both terror and anticipation through him, but when I'd inquired about the newot, his expression had become wholly full of anticipation alone. I'd gotten the newot for only one credit—currency far from enough for a life. But his freedom will make Marion happy. I want to see her smile. It is clear her life has been full of disappointment and pain thus far. I want to do everything to change that.

And…I want her to *like* me.

It's a need that's growing as fast as my desire for her. I know nothing about courting humans. I am sure I will make a mess of it before I get it right. But I cannot be impatient. She is not Atari. I must remind myself of this many times.

Gripping the side of my coat so he can keep close to me, the newot tugs once more, garnering a lifted eyebrow from me.

He is a nervous, frail thing. No garments on his back except for the piece of cloth tied around his nether regions to give him some modesty. There are also scars. Dull marks now faint against his skin.

I can tell he had been beaten before. Many times.

"What is your name, newot?"

"Klaok," he says, his voice trembling.

"And what is the matter, Klaok?"

"We go the wrong way…new master." We both know I will never be his master. That role has already been taken and I am sure he knows it can never be replaced. Maybe it is his size…or his helplessness…but my eyes soften at the fact he is trying.

"This is the way to the inn. I bring you to the female that wished for your freedom."

He gulps and we continue on, weaving through the throng toward the inn. But then I feel him tug on my cloak again.

"Klaok?"

"Wrong way, master." He is visibly shivering now, and I pause, looking down at him.

"Explain."

"Evil goes this way," he says, sniffing the air. "Klaok smells strong evil."

My gaze narrows. Newots have an enviable sense of smell. It is probably their only defense mechanism. I should heed his warning.

"Tell me," I say. "What do you smell?"

His large eyes dart around us as he shuffles closer to me, his hand tightening on my cloak.

"Evil Khuru," he says. "Evil, evil Khuru."

His words send a chill through me, so much so that I don't see or hear anything around me as I turn and continue toward the inn, almost running all the way.

He might be wrong. But as soon as I enter the inn, I know something is amiss.

The sparse furnishings are strewn across the floor, and the innkeeper's counter is smashed.

The metal box with the food falls from my hands as I lift my head to look up the stairs to the second level.

Marion.

I almost trip over the innkeeper's body as I head for the stairs, a fear I never knew before crawling up my spine.

Marion's in danger.

"I tried to stop them," the innkeeper says, his voice the only thing causing me to pause.

I crouch to look at him.

His face is covered in his own lifeblood and his four legs lie limp, as if they have been broken.

"Stop *who?*" Anger is spreading through my blood so fast, I can feel my pulse rising.

He chokes on his lifeblood as he grips his midsection. "The Khuru…" He breathes. "…and the velushan."

Rage fills me so suddenly that my eyes burn red.

"Where are they?" I growl.

The innkeeper raises a weak hand and points upward.

Hope shoots through me.

They are still here. That means there is still time to save Marion.

"Wait here," I tell Klaok. "Tend to him."

Klaok nods and I'm bounding up the stairs in the next moment, my steps fast but light enough that I know the brutes won't hear my approach.

The door to the room is wide open and I freeze at the entrance at the scene in front of me.

"Come to me, soft one. I should have won you at the auction if that stranger had not stolen you away from me," the velushan hisses, his arms reaching for my Marion.

There is fear in her eyes as she backs away till her back hits the wall, but there is something else in her eyes as well. Defiance.

But she is cornered. Outnumbered.

Not anymore. I am here, and no one in the room has noticed my arrival.

"Fuck. You!" Marion spits. "Do you really think I will just come with you because you *ask* me to? You're working with that monster!" Her eyes fly to the Khuru and at that moment, she sees me.

But unlike what most females would do in this situation, Marion doesn't scream and run to me, giving my advantage away. Instead, her gaze flicks back to the Khuru.

"You ugly piece of shit! You killed them!" she screams at the Khuru. "They didn't deserve it, yet you killed them all. You murderer!"

"Grab hold of it before I snap its neck," the Khuru replies, and the velushan moves to grab Marion.

Marion ducks, catching his arm in the folds of the cloak, and the velushan lets out a sound of surprise.

"You're not taking me anywhere," Marion growls.

For a moment, she looks completely different from the female I rescued. This is a part of her that wasn't revealed before.

This rage.

This will to fight…

It makes my life organ swell for her even more.

The velushan, being only a little bigger than she is, is caught off guard and stumbles into the wall. Marion takes the opportunity to kick him in the back before spinning away from him, sliding over the sleeping area, and putting some distance between them.

"You are mine!" the velushan shouts, his words making me see red.

"I would die first!" Marion screams back.

As the Khuru growls, his first step toward her is halted as my hand closes over his shoulder.

"It would be wise if you halt your steps. I can't promise I will be gentle if you go even a foot nearer to her," I say.

"Gentle?" He stiffens and turns, green eyes going almost pupil-less as they land on me.

"Yes," I reply. "With your death."

He doesn't get the chance to swing his tail to hit me and make me lose my balance. I already know Khuru fighting tactics and my fist lands in his nose, stunning him, before his tail can move.

He staggers backward, hitting the bath and almost losing his balance. I help him with that, another fist connecting with his jaw sends him crashing into the tub.

There is a hiss to my right as the velushan comes to his senses. He rushes for Marion and in her shock watching me, she doesn't move quickly enough.

He grabs her and her surprised scream pierces the air.

One arm around her neck, he pulls her backward across the sleeping area, his eyes on me.

Marion thrashes, her arm flailing as she tries to hit her assailant and when I take a step in her direction, her eyes widen as she screams my name.

"Aqnar! Behind you!"

I spin in time to miss the Khuru's attack, the air slicing above my head as I duck. The Khuru's sharp blade glistens in the light.

Annoying.

I am done playing games with this brute. He is the one that brought my mate here to this shithole planet. He is the one that got the Zedice to sell her.

He has brought her pain. And I will erase it by erasing him.

Spinning with a kick, my boot lands on the Khuru's wrist and he lets out a yelp of pain as his blade falls.

I'm standing before he can recover, my fist locked around his throat as I drive him back into the wall.

Behind me, the velushan yelps, and I glance to see Marion has sunk her small teeth into the arm he has around her neck.

He releases her, but not before he strikes her hard with his other arm.

"Worthless female!" he shouts.

As Marion falls to the floor, I know I must finish this quickly.

I turn back to the Khuru in my grasp, my anger burning a red fire that will consume us both if I don't release it.

"You," I growl.

"Who are you?" he asks, and when I tilt my head enough for him to see my face, his expression changes to one of fear.

"A-An Atari? What are you doing here?!"

My nostrils flare. "You chose the wrong female to qef with."

His eyes go pale just before I squeeze and twist. The snap of his neck is loud as both my fists collapse his throat.

His body goes limp almost immediately and I let it drop to the floor just as a rush of footsteps sounds behind me.

But the velushan isn't fast enough. I spin just in time to grab him by the neck as he reaches the door.

"Your turn."

He hisses, his fangs descending and dripping toxin that will leave me paralyzed if he manages to sink his teeth into my skin. Rage burns through me. Those are the same fangs he'd use to pierce my Marion. The same toxin he'd flood into her system so she couldn't move while he impregnated her with his seed.

The thoughts send white-hot rage through me, and I squeeze his neck so hard, his tongue lolls out and he gasps for air.

"I am sorry!" he squeals. "She is yours. You paid for her."

"Seems you didn't think so when you found your way here," I growl. "Let me remind you."

I pull him backward as I grab the Khuru's knife from the floor.

Pressing the scum into the wall, I look him in the eyes. He pales when he recognizes me as Atari.

"You were going to paralyze her. *Impregnate* her."

He stutters, unable to think of a lie to save himself. My nostrils flare, the edges of my mouth quivering as I snarl at him.

"You wanted to breed my mate."

His eyes widen some more.

"I didn't know—"

His words suddenly stop as I bury the blade into his midsection and let him go. He looks down at the hilt as his body slowly slides to the floor. And I don't care. White-hot rage is consuming me. The only thing that pulls me to the surface is the fact that Marion has not risen from where she had fallen.

She is still on the floor and that fear that crawled up my spine when I first entered the inn crawls right back.

I rush toward her, my life organ beating an irregular, unfamiliar beat.

"Marion!"

I round the resting area to see her body slumped on the floor and panic shoots through me at the sight of her.

I just found her. I cannot lose her now.

18

Marion

My head feels foggy. Heavy. Like a block of iron I cannot lift. And there's an ache in my jaw, a new fresh one. I lift my hand to brush against it, hissing as my fingers make contact with my skin.

"Oh, thank the gods."

The voice coming from directly above me makes me startle, my eyes flying open to the blurry outline of a large male.

"Marion…" His voice sends shivers all along my skin, and as my vision clears, the golden eyes above me seep with worry.

"Aqnar?" Ouch. So speaking apparently hurts. I wince, my hand flying back to my jaw, but he catches my wrist.

"Don't touch it. It will only make it worse. The balm I applied will begin working soon."

There's a pounding in my head at the sudden onslaught of input into my senses and I frown, trying to regulate myself.

He's braced above me…and I'm flat on my back on the bed.

"Wh-what happened?" My eyes widen as memory of the last few seconds before everything went black comes flashing in my mind. "That guy and the murderer!"

Aqnar makes a deep purring sort of sound, pushing himself even closer to me as he nuzzles my temple with his nose.

"Do not fret. They can harm you no longer. I made sure of that."

My eyes still dart toward the door.

It's closed now and we are once again alone.

"What happened to them?"

Aqnar lifts his head so he's looking down at me, his face so close, I can see the threads of bronze that spun his skin.

There's a look in his eyes that makes me know whatever he's about to say is going to send chills down my spine.

"They no longer exist." He says it without remorse, and I realize at that moment that I'm looking into the face of a male who just killed two others to save *my* life. My heart gives one hard thump against my chest, and I lift my hand to cradle the jaw of this handsome being that's looking down at me. Tears fill my eyes, tears I refuse to let fall, but Aqnar notices anyway.

A look I can't read passes over his features. "You…feel sadness for their deaths? You wished I had let them live…"

I swallow down the lump forming in my throat.

"No." I shake my head, and another confusing expression passes over his face. "I…Aqnar…*you almost died.*"

His eyes widen ever so slightly.

"I don't give a shit about that cunt and his friend," I choke, a stubborn tear finding itself winding down my cheek. Aqnar braces on his elbow and uses a finger to wipe it away. "But he almost killed you because you were distracted trying to protect *me*. I don't know what I'd have done if you'd died *because* of me."

"You don't?" he whispers.

I choke on another sob mixed in with a laugh. "Of course I don't. I still haven't paid you back yet. And I owe you…" *ohmyfuckingGod* "I owe you *everything.*"

I pause. Reality hitting me like a brick. I can't deny it. Those words I just uttered are true.

I owe Aqnar *everything*.

"Marion…" My name's rough on his lips, as if it's been grated out with the way his voice has become raspy and deep.

I don't get a warning before his head dips, his lips closing over mine.

The feel of his lips sends a lightning bolt right through me, jerking me back into my body and I sob into his mouth.

But there's nothing sorrowful about what his tongue is doing with mine. Nothing remotely gentle either. All I can feel is unbridled need. *Want.* And for once, I silence my mind and wrap my arm around this man. I let him kiss me.

I let his tongue fuck my mouth, allowing it to delve deep, seeking the length of mine before he wraps his own tongue around it. I moan against his lips, unable to help myself before Aqnar pulls his tongue back and sucks mine into his mouth. My center clenches, pulling a groan from deep within me as my back arches toward him.

The moment our lips break, I pant his name. "Aqnar…"

Gazing up into his eyes, I see nothing resembling the male that held me earlier and joked about me being afraid of acknowledging his cock.

The male staring down at me now looks like he is starved, and all he wants to do is consume. *Me.*

"Aqnar?" A chill goes through me, a delicious one that coalesces at my nipples, making them hard, before swirling down my belly to settle at the nub between my folds.

"Aqnar…" I say his name again, but whatever has possessed him does not give him leave. And looking at him, frozen above me, he is staring at me like a man starved would look at meat dangling before his face. I instinctively tilt my head back, baring my neck to him.

Aqnar growls enough that his fangs bare. They drip as he stares at me. There is the sound of tearing beside my head and I slide my gaze to see his hands gripping the bedding beneath us. And tearing it. He's dug his hands in so deep, he's ripping the fabric to shreds.

I don't know what the fuck is happening. All I know is that I am not scared, and I should be! But this male before me has saved my life twice now and been nothing but good to me. I can't resist the urges going through my body, so hard that every hair on my skin is standing on end.

"Aqnar…" I say his name again.

Logic says I should get the fuck out of here. Logic says I should exit while I still have the chance, while he is frozen above me, just staring at me, doing nothing but watching me like a wild cat watching its prey.

But even with his cloak on, I can see that every muscle in his arms is bunched.

He may not be moving, but I *can't*. Every instinct tells me that if I move even an inch, *something* will happen. So I stay still, not even daring to breathe as I stare up into the eyes of this male. Hoping he will give me what my body's begging for, but my mind won't acknowledge.

For that need gathering between my thighs, that slick, that warmth to be sated…

"Marion," he rasps.

I lick my lips and the corners of his tremble, his fangs seeming to grow longer as I watch them with widening eyes.

"Yes?" I whisper.

"You should run."

I swallow hard, watching him. "Yes…I should." I agree.

But I don't move. It is only when his eyes cloud over, the golden storm turning into a black one, that my survival instincts finally kick in.

The color change sends a jolt of excitement straight through me, culminating in my clit, and even as I brace on my elbow, twisting my body so I can dart from underneath him, I'm very aware that what's coursing through me is not fear.

It's *anticipation*.

I don't get far. I don't even get off the bed before I'm thrown on my back and Aqnar bears down at me, snarling so low and into my face that his nose brushes against mine.

I pant, my pussy throbbing and clenching on nothing.

"Aq—!"

His lips close over mine once more.

Not an exploratory kiss, but one that ravages me and leaves me panting. A low moan escapes me as he takes my mouth, his fist tangling in my hair as he tilts my head back.

"Marion…" he growls. "I cannot wait. Not after almost losing you."

Cannot wait for what?

"Tell me you feel it, too. Tell me you want this as badly as I do. It has only been a short time, but I am already burning for you."

I can only moan as his tongue slides deep into my mouth, rendering me speechless. His words send fresh need between my legs, making me clench my thighs tight as his kiss sends me close to the edge.

I can hardly believe what I'm hearing him say, but I would be a fool to deny that my body isn't singing underneath his touch.

Somehow, he manages to shed his cloak, only breaking our kiss at the last moment as he pulls it over his head.

Panting, I stare up at him. Irises no longer gold, the darkness in his eyes makes it seem as if he has no pupils. The sight only sends another delicious shiver through me.

"You," he says. And some invisible demon I cannot see makes his voice sound even deeper.

When Aqnar speaks, it is like he wants to possess me. And maybe that's exactly what he wants to do, with his eyes changed like that.

I swallow hard, forcing down the anticipation balling in my throat, while very aware of the wetness that's gathering in between my folds.

"Marion…" My name's said in that same deep, possessive, god-like way, and I shiver again. "I cannot stay, Marion."

His eyes flick from gold to black as if there is a war raging within him.

"Why?" I whisper.

Those eyes assault me immediately, and the darkness within them grows deeper at the sound of my voice, as if looking down into my face has made him even more possessed.

"Because," he leans in, coming once again so close, I feel the brush of his breath over my nose. "Because I almost lost you…and the only instinct I have right now is to make sure you're marked."

My heart stutters. "Marked?"

"By *me*," he says. The muscles in his arms clench, as if he's trying his best not to touch me but slowly losing the battle. My clit throbs, begging for me to reach down and touch it. Better yet, for *him* to reach down and touch it.

But even I know enough about alien cultures to know that in some species, only *mates* mark each other—usually the male branding the female as his.

Again, the thought should make me concerned. Instead, another thick drop of need flows through me.

Aqnar sniffs the air and growls. His teeth clench and his lips pull back as he faces me. It's a sound that would make anyone afraid. Instead, it is one that makes the nectar flowing between my thighs increase tenfold.

I have fucking lost my will to survive. But I can't think of a better way to die.

He suddenly closes the distance, his lips pressing into mine, and a strangled moan leaves my lips. My hand reaches for his hair, threading through the soft strands as I pull him to me.

It's a kiss that leaves me breathless. A kiss that makes me want for more. Aqnar's tongue moves in my mouth as if he is dying and my kiss is the only thing that will save him.

"Marion," he groans against my lips. "I want to take this slow...*for you*. But by the gods of Atar...you tempt me."

"Me?"

He groans, pulling his lips away from mine, his mouth nibbling against my skin as he makes his way toward my ear.

"Yes," he growls., snarling by my ear, a sound that makes my pussy quiver.

His tongue flicks against my ear and he groans as he kisses a trail down my neck, stopping once to inhale deeply.

Another groan leaves him and there is an answering throb from my clit. Me? I'm the one turning him on so much? The thought is both flattering and intoxicating.

"By the gods," he whispers into my neck. "Take it slow. Humans do not mate like Atari do." But his voice is so low, it's like he's talking to himself and not to me.

When he repeats it one more time, I'm convinced he's trying to calm himself down.

"Slow," he groans, but his head dips, his lips skimming my collar-bone as he inhales deeply one more time.

"What if," I lick my lips, unable to believe what I'm about to say next. "What if I just tell you to stop if I get uncomfortable?"

His head snaps up so he can look at me and his gaze flicks from black to gold, then black again.

He watches me for a few moments, his bottom lip thinning as he pulls it into his mouth and bites down hard enough for me to see his fangs. A trickle of blood from where he broke his skin forms at the corner of his lips, but he ignores it.

"You underestimate my need for you," is all he says.

"I…I don't think…"

'I don't think so' is what I want to say, but when he pulls me closer to him, bringing my body down as one hand circles my hips and grabs my ass, I get to feel what he means.

Rod-like hardness presses hard against his trou and, in effect, hard against me. I feel it grow even larger as the heat between my thighs presses against it.

"But I would be mad not to take what you offer," he finishes.

Aqnar growls and brings us higher on the bed. With one hand, he pulls the cloak I'm wearing high, revealing the tunic underneath. Cool air meets the exposed parts of my skin. When he disappears beneath the cloak, going out of view, I try to sit up. But I'm unable to move as he immediately reaches up and pins my shoulders back.

"Stay," he growls, and, as if commanded by his voice, my body stills, surrendering me as an offering to him.

His hands move, and I wonder what he's about to do when my skin tingles at my hips. He lifts the hem of the tunic before his fingers dig into the waist of the box shorts, pulling them down in one swift movement.

I yelp, my legs coming together out of pure instinct, the thought that he's now face-to-face with my naked cunt making my cheeks flash red.

"Aqnar…"

"Want me to stop?" His deep voice booms from underneath the cloak and I stare at the thick fabric. "Don't say yes," he adds.

I almost chuckle. And I would have if more need didn't shoot through me and cause me to shudder. My throat feels thick as I answer him.

"N-no."

Aqnar pries my legs open without my resistance. His hands move down my legs until I feel his fingers spread over the apex of my thighs. His thumbs brush down either side of my outer lips, so, so close, I'm sure they've already gathered some of my slick on their tips.

I feel his hot breath against my flesh just seconds later.

A million thoughts flash into my head. I didn't shave. My dark curly forest is down there. But when I feel him press his nose into it, my whole body quakes. The thought of my pussy pressed against his face, the *feel* of it, has another gush of warmth going through me.

I moan without meaning to.

Aqnar growls as if he scents it and I wonder if he can, because his finger dips to my entrance, swirling around the wetness there.

"Marion..." he groans, my name vibrating against my pussy lips, rattling my clit like a vibrator would.

"Shit," I whisper, another warm gush going through me. Fuck. I've never been so turned on in my life. It's been a long time since I've done anything with anyone intimately, and that's clear. I feel like putty and this man hasn't done anything to me yet.

"I'm sorry, Marion..."

I hear his voice, but it's almost like it's far away. Sorry? Sorry for what? I expect him to pull away and for my fears to be validated. Instead, he pushes his nose into my clit. "But I can't resist."

That's all the warning I get. That sweet low rumble of his voice, his breath against my folds, before I feel the cool swipe of his tongue over my clit.

Oh fuck.

I jerk so hard, if he wasn't holding me down, I might have levitated. The moan that leaves my lips is primal, *needy*, and it's matched with a deep rumble of his own.

"Aqnar," I pant.

He swipes his tongue right up through me again, the tip dipping into my center before he brings it right up through my folds and over the throbbing bud of my clit.

His voice is muffled as he speaks. "Gods save me. You taste so good."

His praise only makes me jerk against him again, pushing my clit against his face, and he laps at it with abandon, the moans rumbling past his lips like background music that is slowly sending me over the edge.

Aqnar spreads my legs further apart, opening me to him. I'm so wet, I can hear the lapping sounds as he devours his meal. My whole cunt feels swollen and wet, as if desire has filled me and gathered there, and within a few seconds, I'm shivering with pleasure, unable to control myself.

Aqnar lifts a hand, running it up my body and underneath the tunic until it closes over a breast.

I hiss at the sensation the flick of his finger on my nipple sends. My breasts feel big and swollen, the nipples sensitive, as if my body's preparing for something...or *begging* for something...I don't know which. Probably the latter, because I scream his name, mildly aware that anyone outside this room might hear my cries. But I don't care.

The need to come, the urge to reach orgasm, makes my body feverish. My pussy clenches on nothing, desperate to be filled. And, as if Aqnar can hear her cries, he moves his tongue lower and pushes into that tight little needy hole.

"Fuuuck!" I scream, shamelessly pushing my hips down so he can go deeper. I'm gripping the bedding with my hand, my eyes wide as I feel the thick muscle of his tongue flex inside me.

Aqnar releases a groan of pleasure, grasping my ass with one hand as he pulls me down on his face. The other hand grasps my breast within his palm before he pinches my nipple just hard enough for me to feel it.

My eyes roll over, the orgasm crashing through me so hard that I stiffen, a scream of pleasure leaving my lips. I shudder against him as that freight-train high keeps going through me and my mind swirls when I feel his tongue still moving inside me.

"Aqnar," I pant. It's so good. So, so good. It feels like my release pulls all my energy, taking everything I have, right down to my toes.

He slips his tongue out slowly, but when I think he will rise and push his cock into my face for me to return the favor, he doesn't. And I wouldn't even be mad. I want to taste him.

Need to.

Instead, I feel sweet, light kisses on the inside of my thigh.

"More?"

At first, I wonder if I hear right.

"More?" I pant the word.

"Are you ready for more, my sweet mate?"

Mate?

I must have said that out loud because he nuzzles my clit with his nose, causing me to shiver some more.

"My *ari*," he says. "I felt the call of the bond the moment I held you in my arms. I just didn't know it yet."

I blink into the dark ceiling above, my chest heaving as I listen to his words. Things are a little clearer now and…oh my god…I think I've made a horrible mistake.

"Aqnar?"

At the sound of his name, Aqnar rises from under my cloak, the color of his eyes warming to a rich gold as they meet mine. They're not black anymore, but they're still ravenous. He licks his lips, his tongue flicking over his fangs and his mouth, where the sheen of my slick remains.

I have to focus on the cloak in order to pull my eyes away.

"You said you were coming for us…me and the other women who were on that cruise," I say. "Why?" My voice sounds thick now, thick with need I'm too afraid to acknowledge.

He told me before that we were brides. I guess I didn't believe him. But now…now he's calling me his mate.

"Your government struck a deal with mine. We were to collect you, so you could live on Atar and become—"

I have to lift my gaze back to his, to see why he's stopped so suddenly. All I see is a slight dimming of his eyes.

"Become what?" I whisper.

He doesn't answer...he just stares at me.

"This is not how you were supposed to be introduced to this...I do not want to create a wound I cannot heal."

Fisting the cloak tightly in my hand, I drop my gaze once more. I think I already know what he's about to say.

"Tell me," I whisper. "Please..."

After a few more moments, he continues.

"Mates," he says. "We hoped introducing you to our society would provide you with a better life and reduce the strain on our population. We have many...unmated males."

"Mates." A chill goes down my spine.

"Yes, my ari. *Mates*. We wondered if it was possible because your kind is genetically close to Atari, but we weren't quite sure."

My tongue feels thick in my mouth. "And you're sure now?"

His gaze drops to my lips. "Yes..."

"Aqnar," I swallow hard. "What's an 'ari'?"

His gaze meets mine again and I'm struck by the intensity of it.

"*Ari* means mate, Marion...and *you* are *my ari*."

That hole that's opened up in my stomach, the one threatening to swallow me whole, has just gotten ten times bigger.

"You are the other part my soul has been searching this whole time for," Aqnar continues, unaware of the dread and sorrow slowly creeping through me. "And I couldn't have asked for the fates to give me a better female."

I stiffen, his words ricocheting in my head. Oh my god...this explains so much.

"You think I'm your mate," I whisper.

His kindness. The way he's protected me. Everything he's done so far...it's because he thinks I'm something more than I am.

A coldness is slowly settling over me that I do not like. One that makes me pull into myself as I'm hit with a big box of bills from reality and I have to pay up.

"You *are* my mate," he rumbles. "You are human. You might not sense it like I do. But of this, I am sure."

His words only increase a slow burning in my chest. With every high, there is a crash. And my world is crashing down.

There's a pain in my heart. One that makes my belly cramp inwards and I have to breathe deep.

"Marion?"

I can't even answer him. It suddenly hurts too much.

Mate?

I can't be his mate. How can I, when I'm not even deemed suitable for my own kind?

19

Aqnar

I felt the change in her even before I lifted my head from the warmth of her sweet cunt. My mate is hurting.

My mate. The thought sends a surge of possession and need through me. But she is hurting…*and I am the cause.*

She eases up on her elbow, pulling away from me as she squeezes her legs together.

"Aqnar…I…"

Something akin to fear crawls up my spine.

Did I hurt her? Nip her with my fangs?

I tried to be careful. I tried to go slow. But her sweet nectar was like the strongest drug. Even now, thinking about it, I want more, and my cock grows hard in my trou at the thought of pushing my tongue into that tight little hole once again.

I lean toward her, and her gaze drops from mine, sadness a clear emotion flooding across her features.

I am about to ask if I hurt her when there is a sound at the door.

Immediately, the skin along my spine tingles, a snarl rising on my lips. My mate is vulnerable, and there is an intruder at the door. But when no one barges in, I manage to control my urge to destroy any threat.

Threats don't knock.

And then I remember…the newot. I'd left him on the lower floor watching over the hurt innkeeper. Stronger than he looks, he'd pulled away the bodies of the slain scum while I'd stayed by Marion's side. I'd forgotten about him.

"Klaok?" I call his name and the door opens slowly, his too-large head popping in.

"Master…" he says.

"I am not your master, Klaok." My gaze flicks to my mate and her expression of surprise has temporarily hidden the sadness that was creeping into her eyes. "*She* is."

Marion's eyes grow larger as she glances at me.

"She was taken…like Klaok was," he says. "Klaok remembers her."

For a moment, he goes out of view and then reappears with the metal box of food in his arms. He takes a few tentative steps forward, ignoring me as his gaze remains on Marion.

Setting the box at the foot of the bed, he stands and wrings his hands as he looks at her.

I understand his nervousness. She is a beauty. Her pale eyes, such a contrast to her dark hair. Her perfect soft skin… I have no doubt the velushan wasn't the only one who wanted to get her into his harem. Just the thought makes me inch a little closer to her.

Marion reaches her hand toward Klaok, palm upward.

"Hello," she whispers.

His ears flick and he looks at me. A thrill goes through me. Even though I haven't marked her yet, he can smell her arousal, see the sheen of it on my lips. He knows she is mine and will not approach my mate without first asking for approval. I have not marked her yet. But even though I am not like some Atari, who will attack anyone who comes close to their mate before the bond is solidified, I enjoy that even he, as a newot, acknowledges my claim.

Marion is *mine*.

When I nod, Klaok moves forward. He looks at her outstretched hand, not sure of what to do. It is a human custom we had to learn when we met with the New Earth leaders. One that's often used for greeting. A shake of hands, they call it. But Klaok has never been to New Earth. Marion may be the first human he has ever encountered.

His hesitation is obvious, and when Marion is just about to pull her hand away, he moves forward and puts his entire forehead into her palm.

Marion makes a small sound of surprise. One that has my mind immediately going back to moments before. The sweet small sounds she made while my tongue moved between her sweet slit.

I want to hear them again. I want to hear her cry my name as I lap at her cunt and drink her juices.

"It is a pleasure to meet you, new master," Klaok says.

Marion's eyes widen again and a surprised laugh escapes her throat. I blink at her.

This may well be the first time I've heard her genuine sound of happiness. It is an addictive sound.

"I-I'm not your master," she says.

Klaok's head immediately snaps up, his ears falling back against his head, his eyes growing bigger, and he seems to shrink into himself.

"You do not wish to keep Klaok?" he says. His voice is so dejected, it's evident that immediate guilt consumes Marion.

I growl. He's making her sadder than before, and I have not yet discovered why she withdrew from me. I do not want her tears. I want more of her laughter.

"Oh, I—." She glances at me for help. "I didn't say that. Do you want me to keep you? I thought you'd want to be free. How—" She glances at me again. "How did you even end up here?"

"Master came and bought Klaok's life."

I groan at his choice of words and Marion utters a sad sort of laugh.

"I guess it's not a nice way to put it," she says, "but if I want to face the music, it's the exact thing he's done for me. It's why I have to pay him back." She meets my gaze. "I can't keep accepting his kindness and giving nothing back in return."

Something inside of me cringes and I want to reach for her. I want to tell her she owes me nothing. That my soul has been searching for its other half for what feels like eons and that now that I've found her, I want nothing more. I want to tell her she's already given me more than she could ever dream. There is no question about it. I know she will make me the happiest male to have ever existed. Mate bonds never fail. Mate bonds are true, and for once, I have hope. Hope for a female. Hope for a *lover*. Hope for a mate of my own.

"Klaok's fate was once dire before master arrived," Klaok continues, breaking into my thoughts. At his words, Marion pulls her attention away from me.

"So was mine," she whispers, and once again, I am reminded of the horrors she's been through in this short amount of time. If I could do it all over again... If I could turn back time and arrive before the Khuru did, I would save her from the pain.

"Aqnar," she says, my name rolling off her tongue as if we have known each other for a lifetime...and *I love the sound*. "You returned to the auction room for Klaok? Why?"

Her voice is so soft, I can tell that whatever my answer, it will be important. But I can only tell her the truth.

"Does Klaok's presence make you happy?" I ask. "Do you feel better now that he will have a home? Now that he has been bought and will no longer suffer the torture of being a Zedice's pet?"

Marion's gaze doesn't leave my own and silence fills the room. I wonder what she is thinking, would give anything to find out, but I refrain from prodding her to respond. This female of mine is an introspective one. Wise. And brave. I could have asked the fates for no better.

But as she stares at me, the corners of her eyes grow wet, and the feeling of dread that had been settling in my gut returns.

"Marion..."

I hate to see those tears. I hate to know I am the cause of them. I want to fix this, whatever I have done. Perhaps...perhaps losing control and tasting her sweet nectar had been a bad decision. Perhaps the wound I've inflicted is no physical one. I do not smell her blood, but that does not mean she's not hurting inside.

I step toward her, wanting nothing more than to pull her into my arms. If only she'll let me.

And she does.

The moment I pull her into my arms, she melts against me, gripping my leathers as she buries her face into my chest.

It is an indescribable feeling, being her comfort...but my life organ aches...for I am also the reason she is in pain.

"Marion," I manage to speak past the hoarseness in my throat. "I have hurt you...please know it was not my intention. I have never...I have never done this before..."

But that is no excuse...

She sobs into my chest.

"No. You don't understand," she sniffles. "I thought you were just doing your duty or something when you saved me. But now, you... you've saved *two* of us from a fate that would have killed us..." Wiping away a tear, she continues. "It feels like this is all a dream. Like I died on that ship with all the other women and my soul's conjured *you.*"

I can feel the pain in her voice and now that I know where it stems from, I'm partially relieved and saddened. When I pull her even closer to me, she allows me to. Leaning closer, I place a soft kiss on her forehead. She sniffles and grips my arm that's around her.

"This is a dream. And I don't want to wake up."

My female hurts. And I do not know how to fix it. I realize now that it is not only the tragedy she experienced that affects her but her time on her planet too. New Earth has treated my mate unfairly. Invisible scars have formed deep trenches that affect her even now. I would raze it to the ground if I could.

"Female master is saddened," Klaok suddenly says. "Klaok wishes to make the female master happy. Klaok does not wish to return to the Zedice's lair." His ears are still flattened, his hands clasped, his shoulders folded, making him look even smaller. "Klaok will work very hard to be a good slave. Klaok will do whatever jobs you wish, female master."

A sob breaks from Marion as she reaches for him. But instead of accepting her comfort, he jerks back and freezes, his eyes going wide. Marion pauses too, her outstretched hand halting in the air.

He looks at it with fear, and they stare wide-eyed at each other, neither sure what move to make. When he realizes she's not trying to harm him, he allows her to rest her hand over his still-clasped and much smaller ones.

"I don't want a slave, Klaok," Marion says. Klaok's eyes widen even more, fear filling them, and Marion continues quickly. "I want a *friend*."

Klaok's ears perk off the sides of his head and he just stares at her for a few moments. And, almost unnoticeably, his skin changes, his paleness becoming warmer, pinker.

"A *friend*?" he whispers.

"Yes." Marion nods, and once again I am impressed by the pureness of this female. She doesn't know, but she just told the little newot that she will be his family. Newots don't differentiate between the two...but a family is exactly what the creature needs.

"Klaok has never had a *friend* before." His eyes shimmer before he suddenly throws himself at Marion, jumping onto the bed as his arms stretch to hug her. Tears well in her eyes again and I resist the urge to wipe them away. She looks up at me, those pale eyes meeting mine.

"You did this. You went and got Klaok. You took care of the two scumbags that came to take me away. You've done all this for *me*, so my heart can be less burdened. So I can be *happy*." As she turns to my chest, resting her head there, words whisper from her mouth that I'm not sure she knows I hear.

"I wonder if you know how much you've saved us both?"

20

Marion

As we get ready to leave Ockorius III, Aqnar has been nothing but understanding of my silence. Even though I do not speak, he doesn't pry. He doesn't tell me how I should feel and he doesn't act as if I'm inconveniencing him either.

All evidence that he's just…everything I've ever wanted.

As we walk through the busy streets of this godforsaken city, he holds me close. Not once has his arm across my shoulder moved, and even though I'm well-hidden underneath the cloak, his presence by my side brings me confidence.

Even Klaok walks close by him, hiding under Aqnar's large cloak. It is clear the little newot can sense the strength and safety Aqnar provides.

Now, the streets seem even busier than the first time I walked through them. When I arrived here, I was pulled by that murderer like cattle behind him. Now I am leaving, and I am walking by the side of a fearless male—one any woman would die to have.

Shit.

What am I going to do?

I can't be his mate. I've lived my life being reminded at every turn that I am not "mateable". Not "weddable". Not worthy of making a family with anyone, much less a *god* from Atar.

FUCK.

"But that doesn't mean you are not his mate."

What?

I blink and almost stumble into the people walking in front of us. It's a good thing they don't notice because the last thing I want to do is bring attention to us.

"Who said that?" I glance around, but it's impossible to find the speaker. Everyone's head is held straight, minding their business, like drones heading to a beehive.

"Marion?" Aqnar bends so he can speak close to my ear. "Is everything alright?"

I nod, a little flustered. "Yes…I'm okay." I glance around us again, but there is no one there. Maybe I imagined it.

"It is me, Klaok."

My eyes bug out and I spot Klaok's face as he pushes his head from under Aqnar's cloak. I stare at him, almost stumbling again but managing to remain upright all because of Aqnar's hold on me.

"Klaok?" I whisper.

"Aye, master," he says…*in my mind!*

"Newots usually only mind-speak only with others of our kind," he says. *"But master said Klaok is her friend. Klaok will speak to her like this."*

"Klaok…" I whisper, shock hindering any other response. I have never had another being in my mind before. The effect is…strange.

"Master is Atari," he continues, as if he can hear me just fine, even though I whispered to him. *"You will know he is your mate when he marks you."*

His words send a shiver down my spine, and I glance from under the hood of the cloak, barely catching sight of Aqnar's chin. He tilts his head to look down at me, the upper portion of his face hidden in shadow, before he bends so he can speak into my ear again.

"Do not fear…we will arrive at my cruiser soon."

I gulp and nod as if that's the reason my heart's thumping too fast, my gaze flicking to Klaok. The newot smiles at me.

"How do you know?" I whisper, turning my head forward so Aqnar doesn't see that I am speaking.

"Klaok knows he is weak. Klaok must know everything about worlds close to his homeworld. Klaok must know how to protect himself."

Well, shit. I glance at him but manage to keep my face straight. I wonder what else he knows but maybe, in time, I will find out. What he said about Aqnar marking me though…

"The mark seals the bond," he says, his voice almost a whisper in my mind.

"And if he marks me and there is no bond?" I whisper back.

As we walk, Aqnar guides us from the main thoroughfare down a side street.

"Almost there," he says. I nod, my gaze flicking to Klaok.

I'm fully aware he hasn't answered my last question, and that does nothing but raise the anxiety already settled in my belly.

By the time we get to his cruiser, I'm left with one big decision.

Go with Aqnar…or tell him to leave me someplace other than New Earth. Or…do what this little man-creature is telling me I should do.

The decision is made when Aqnar opens the cruiser's doors and gestures to the inside.

"It's small," he says. "But it will get us home."

My heart aches. *Home.* Get *us* home. Both of us. As if I already belong there.

I swallow past the lump in my throat as he lifts me and hops up into the cruiser with ease. When Klaok hops in behind him and the door closes, locking us in, Aqnar takes off the hood of his cloak and sets me on my feet.

"Steady?" he asks. I nod, not trusting my voice. My eyes meet Klaok's and there is a knowing look in the newot's gaze.

"I will bring us into orbit and then set course for Atar," Aqnar says, glancing back at me. "But if you wish to go somewhere else, I will take you there."

My heart aches some more and I manage to shake my head. I don't even know where else I would go if not Atar. I don't have many choices…and a part of me doesn't want any choice at all. What Aqnar is offering is what I want.

I glance back at Klaok and he is still watching me.

Let him mark me, I think to myself, fisting my cloak so tightly, the fibers feel hard in my palm.

As Aqnar turns to the control panel, he activates something and a second seat unfolds behind me. I sit, and while the straps are secured, all I can think about are those words. *Let him mark me.*

Why does the thought terrify me so?

Because you're scared of the one thing that has held you back all your life. The thought comes so suddenly and so clearly, that I glance in Klaok's direction. But he has moved to sit at the front on Aqnar's leg, holding on to him for support as the engine engages and the cruiser begins to hum. It is not him who has spoken to me. The thought is my own.

"Hold on," Aqnar says, glancing back at me. His gaze is warm, but it doesn't calm the sour feeling of anxiety filling my blood.

I nod at him again and brace myself. But takeoff is smooth, much smoother than it was in that cursed ship I went on for the "cruise". Soon, we are high above the factories of Ockorius III.

When we break the atmosphere and start zooming away from the planet, Aqnar releases his seat restraints and stands, allowing Klaok to take his seat.

"She'll take us to Atar now," he says.

A shudder goes through me.

I know why this scares me so much. Lifting my arm, I rub my nub underneath the cloak. As Aqnar approaches me, I feel that fear as clearly as if it has its claws around me.

I fear this isn't real. Scared of him marking me and this bond he believes is there failing. I'm scared, because all my life, I've been told I don't deserve this exact thing.

I'm a coward.

As Aqnar releases my seat restraints and pulls me into his arms, I let him, unable to fight against the pull. He feels too good. He feels…right.

And as he sets the seat back into the cruiser's side and settles onto the floor, pulling me against his chest, I want to cry at how good it feels to be held by him.

He holds me there, not forcing me to speak, but allowing the silence to surround us as I settle in his arms.

Space is cold. I can feel the temperature drop and the cruiser's automatic adjustment as we head into the unknown. But the warmth at my back, the strength of the arms holding me, is all I focus on. I focus on him. And when the cruiser meets some interference and I shudder, he holds me steady, whispering into my hair that I am safe. That I will be alright.

And I *am* safe. I know this. I am sure of it.

Safe enough that I drift to sleep in his arms.

I wake with a start, mildly confused before it all becomes clear. I'm in Aqnar's cruiser, heading *home*. Even though I fell asleep, the big alien that's holding me against him hasn't moved. He's stayed cradling me on the floor, never leaving my side as if he doesn't want to let me go.

And...I don't want him to.

"Aqnar?" I whisper and he immediately rubs his cheek against my head, ruffling my hair.

"We are almost there, my *ari*."

I don't think my heart can bloom any more for him.

Resting my hand against his chest, I feel when his breath hitches because of the contact. Only when I keep my hand there does he release a slow breath and keep on breathing. Above, he idly runs a hand through my hair.

We lie here in silence, just the hum of the engine in the background, and for the first time in a while, I feel perfect peace.

It is a pleasant feeling, and I fight the terror in the background of my mind. The one that's asking questions like what will happen when we reach our destination?

When we're back in reality, back in society, and this all turns out to be a mistake?

A crackle on the ship causes Klaok to jump. He hops out of the chair and heads to me, coming to grip my hand.

Aqnar makes a low sound in his throat. "I'm going to have to set some boundaries with this newot," he murmurs so low, I wouldn't have heard if his jaw wasn't right against the side of my head.

I want to giggle, but there's another crackle and the comms activate.

"Aqnar, do you read?"

"I am here, Qhenno," he speaks, and there is another crackle before whoever is contacting us continues.

"You near Atar."

A chuckle rumbles through Aqnar's chest. "I should have known you would be tracking me." He pauses, his gaze falling back to me as he lifts a finger to run down my cheek. "Yes, I near Atar. I have Marion here, safe."

"Marion?" the person asks.

"Yes, my m—the female I found. That is her designation." He pauses again. "Is there a problem?"

"Not on your end, no. But I fear it will take us some time to find the other females the Khuru took. At least you have one safe. It is more than was initially expected from the Khuru."

"Do not lose faith, Qhenno."

There is a grunt as I wait for the person to say more and some guilt tinges inside me. While I've been here comfortably in Aqnar's arms, worrying about my dreams falling apart, who knows what's been happening to the other women?

"Do you think he will find them?" I whisper to Aqnar.

"I promise you, Marion, that we will do our best to find the remaining survivors," Qhenno answers me directly. "Aqnar, once you take the female to the surface, will you join us in the search for the others?"

Aqnar stiffens behind me. "No, I cannot leave Marion alone."

I tilt my head back so I can look at him, shaking my head. I don't want him to shirk his duties because of me—especially when it comes to saving the other women. I open my mouth to protest, but Aqnar's already shaking his head back.

"I'm not leaving you, Marion. Qhenno, Da'red, and Bhihan are more than capable."

His friend makes a sound of surprise. "Since I have known you,

Aqnar, you have never wanted to stay long on the surface. What has changed now?"

Aqnar stares down at me, not answering, and I think he won't until he says, "I think I have found my *ari*."

A delicious shiver goes through me at once more hearing the word. At *knowing* what it means. But the silence of his friend on the line has me holding my breath.

"So soon?" his friend finally asks. "News of this will spread quickly."

Aqnar grunts, just as there is another beep in the ship.

"We near Atar, Qhenno. I am being hailed by the planetary defense system. We must continue this conversation later. May the gods be with you."

"And you, comrade."

There is a click before another voice comes over the intercom.

"Vessel IR-88736, please identify yourself."

Aqnar rises into a fully upright position, bringing me with him. "I apologize my ari, but I must tend to this."

I nod, giving him a nervous smile, and he places a kiss on the top of my head. Pressing a button on the side of the ship, he rises with me as the seat folds out from the wall.

"I know it is cramped, but we will land in a short time."

I nod, watching him as he stretches while speaking directly to the comms as he moves back to the seat in front.

He speaks to whoever is on the other end, relaying codes I don't know the meaning of, and I have nothing to do but to rise and sit in the seat that folded out from the wall. By the time he is finished speaking, I have strapped myself into the small seat with Klaok standing by my legs, his thin arms wrapped around them for stability.

Aqnar glances back at me. "Ready, Marion?"

His voice grew thicker as he spoke my name and warmth floods through me.

I nod. "Ready."

The more time passes, the more this feels like a dream and that feeling doesn't dissipate even as Aqnar takes the controls and we begin to descend.

Outside of the ship, there are vast bodies of water and a tall city rising from the ground. But it looks nothing like New Earth. At least, not the New Earth I'm used to. Everything I see outside is clean, pristine, and perfect.

Golden arches curve around the towering buildings and as we near, I realize the arches are roads. Floating vehicles zoom along them at incredible speeds, and interwoven with these, transparent tubes filled with more pedestrians than I can count wind around the city.

I must have gasped or done something to relay my awe because Aqnar glances back at me, his gaze filling with warmth as soon as his eyes land on me.

"This is Atar?" I ask.

"Yes." He grins. "Your new home."

His gaze softens. "You must be tired. For that reason, I will take you directly to my dwelling and get the medic there. We will deal with the government later."

I nod, more out of shock than because of anything he said. This is too unreal to believe.

The small cruiser moves with ease around the large buildings, and I find myself leaning out of my seat to look out the viewscreen. After prodding me to see if I am willing, Klaok climbs to stand on my lap so he can see outside too. His eyes reflect the wonder in mine.

"Not long now," Aqnar says, but I find his words only send a spike of nervousness through me.

This is already beyond my wildest dreams. Beyond anything I could have imagined.

I'm left in awe; everywhere I look has something else that is new, different...exciting.

Even the animals that I spot, the birds in the skies, and pets on leashes I spy with the pedestrians traveling in the tubes, all look like unique, better versions of the strays that wander on Lower Earth.

"A-are we on the upper levels?" I ask.

"Upper levels?" Aqnar glances at me. "There are no upper levels. What you see is what Atar is. Every major city is like this. Even some towns rival what you see outside."

I'm left dumbstruck once more.

No lower levels…

This is…this is something that will take a long time to get used to.

"So the upper class—"

The shuttle makes one final, smooth turn before lowering onto the rooftop of a flat, broad building.

Around us, the breeze plays with the branches of long palms and trees that grow around the perimeter of the property.

It looks secluded, even though beyond the tree line lies the city we just flew through.

Aqnar rises from his seat and his warm gaze finds me.

"There is no upper class. Apart from the royal family, every citizen is valued the same."

My eyes widen. That thought is as foreign to me as the city I just flew through.

On New Earth, the division of classes is so distinct, one cannot escape it.

There is an expectant sort of look in Aqnar's eyes as he reaches for my seat restraints and releases them.

Without asking, he takes me into his arms, giving Klaok no other option than to stand on his own two feet. Cradling me against his chest, Aqnar steps toward the cruiser's door.

"I can walk—"

"I wish to carry you," he counters, that same look in his eyes.

I try to keep my arm at my side but it's not only uncomfortable but impractical. I end up wrapping my arm around his neck, and Aqnar grunts approval as he exits the shuttle and heads down a set of stairs built into the roof.

It leads directly into the dwelling below and a gasp lodges in my throat.

Aqnar pauses as soon as we are inside.

Pristine white walls border the space as modern furnishings fill the interior.

Gold trim runs along the base of the walls and on most of the furniture, too.

This one room is already ten times bigger than my small apartment back on New Earth and probably worth ten thousand times its value.

I don't realize Aqnar is looking at me, that same expectant yet worried look in his eyes, until my eyes catch his.

"I know it is not much. I have lived here for most of my adult life but have not changed it from the base furnishings. You are welcome to decorate it as you wish."

I blink at him, my eyes widening even more. "Are you kidding me?"

When his expression doesn't change, I realize he is indeed not kidding.

"Your home is...*beautiful*. It would be presumptuous of me to complain or even suggest you change a thing."

Aqnar's lips break into a smile. "Maybe not now, but later. When you are more comfortable. After all, it is your home now, too."

I blink several times, his words ricocheting in what suddenly feels like my empty head as he walks over to the couch and sets me down.

"Rest now. I will contact the medic."

Distantly, I know I nod. And as I watch him move to the wall, activating a sort of communication device and speaking through it, I stare at him.

This is real?

By the entrance, Klaok stands, his face reflecting my exact emotions. Wonder, dismay, unsurety, fear...and hope.

I force myself to focus on him because focusing on everything else is blowing my mind.

"Klaok, why are you standing there like that? Are you okay?"

His large eyes land on me and he takes one tentative step forward, then another, and another, until he is by my side.

"Klaok wishes to know if this is real."

I have to hold back a giggle at how I've been thinking the same thing. And I can't answer him. I want to tell him I'm not quite sure it is. That maybe I *did* survive the trauma of what happened on that ship, and this is my mind's way of protecting me—by making up a world it knows I'll love and not want to part from. And by even conjuring him, Klaok.

Because what Aqnar is telling me is that...this is my life now.

Aqnar finishes the call and heads back over to me, slipping off his cloak and resting it on another seat there. I can't help but notice the sway of his hips in his trou, my gaze slipping to that bulge hidden beneath the fibers.

Shamelessly, my pussy clenches at the thought, memory of his tongue pushing deep inside me almost making me whimper.

"I…" He glances around the room. "I did not prepare for your arrival. I will have to make arrangements. I hardly spend time at this place…and I wasn't expecting to stay here now—much less with company."

He glances at Klaok, whose ears flatten at the sides of his head.

I shift, trying to rise. "We don't want to be a bother—"

Aqnar's eyes snap to mine. "Marion, you are never a bother."

I force a smile, my heart breaking and mending only to break and mend again. "You're making it very hard for me repay you. At this rate, I never will be able to."

"Klaok wishes to repay you too," Klaok butts in, and the look on Aqnar's face only grows more severe.

Leaning down toward me, he braces against the back of the seat and looks me deep in the eye.

"I can only think of one way I'd want you to 'repay' me," he says, that heated gold melting in his eyes. "But that will have to wait till later."

21

Marion

The medic is a rat.

One that walks upright on two legs, is the size of a child, and wears glasses like a human does.

Aqnar insisted he check me over, even though I feel okay. So I squeeze my eyes shut and try to block out the soft pads of his thin fingers as they move over my back.

He's removed the bandage across my back, cleaned the wounds, stitched them up, and put on a new bandage.

"The numbing agent I administered will be more effective and last longer than the one in the ointment you applied," he says to me.

"Mmhm." I nod, only opening one eye to peek at him.

I know I'm probably being unsociable, but I can't get over the fact that he's a ginormous rat. Those things are pests on the lower levels, getting into our food, and contaminating our scarce drinkable water.

"As for the wound on your jaw, I have applied an ointment that will see it healing in a day." He turns to Aqnar. "She is very thin and needs much consistent sustenance and nurturing. It seems she has denied her body of suitable nutrition for the past few years...or longer."

My mouth falls open in shock and I stutter, the words not coming fast enough for me to defend myself before Rat-Doc continues.

"She will also need a prosthetic for that limb."

I groan, my nub burning as if it is also ashamed. It's the first I have thought about it in a while, and I realize it is because Aqnar has not even bothered about it—as if it means nothing to him at all. He doesn't even look at it. And when the medic mentions it, he doesn't glance toward it either. He doesn't see it as some flaw that needs correcting.

That little thing shouldn't make me feel as good as it does.

The medic picks up his things, placing them neatly in his bag before heading toward the door. "I have already deducted payment for my services from your account," he says. "Thank you for your business, Aqnar."

Sitting upright, I readjust my clothing as I watch Aqnar escort him to the door.

"Klaok is happy you are well," Klaok whispers beside me, and I force a smile for his benefit. But inside, my mind's a swirling concoction of nerves and anticipation.

When Aqnar turns after closing the door, he pins me with his gaze.

"I know what you're thinking," he suddenly says. Oh, I don't think he does. All I can think about is what he said. His promise of things that will happen *later*. "But I will accept no payment for ensuring you are well."

I open my mouth to protest, but when his eyes narrow slightly, the words die on my lips, and I find myself smiling instead. I want to tell him it's easy to feel like a burden, but the doorbell rings. It's a soft sound, almost melodious, and Aqnar turns back to the door. It opens as soon as he presses the button and though his large form blocks my view, I can still see the tower of colorful stacked boxes standing there.

The tower moves, staggering forward, the whole thing shaking so much I expect it to topple. Soon it is set down on the small table hovering between the seats, and the small alien who'd been carrying the tower reveals himself. He blinks at me before turning to Aqnar and giving him a bow.

"Please do not forget to leave your impressions of good sustenance on the digiforum," the alien says before promptly leaving.

My eyes are wide as I look at the boxes before me.

"What's…"

Klaok sniffs, his mouth hanging open. He is practically drooling from where he stands.

"Master brings food," he says.

"Food?" I look up at Aqnar.

He shrugs, that lopsided smile that I saw only when he'd been cuddling me in bed reappearing…and so do the memories along with it. My chest warms almost uncomfortably, and I have to rub it underneath the cloak.

"You are hungry. Eat," he says, moving forward to open the first box. He sets it at the edge of the table near where I sit, and I lean forward as the irresistible aroma fills my nose.

In the box is a meal that looks like a gold star restaurant on the upper levels prepared it. My eyes widen as Aqnar crouches before me and spears something that looks like some sort of meat onto a two-pronged fork. He stretches it to my face and slips it into my open mouth.

Flavor spreads across my tongue and I *have* to chew. Even as I do it, Aqnar is watching me with eyes filled with expectation.

"It's delicious," I utter as soon as my mouth is empty.

"Take what you would like," he says to Klaok. "Have your fill."

No longer as hesitant as I am, Klaok grabs the closest box and plops on the floor, digging in immediately.

"You bought this just for us?" I ask. Even to myself, my voice sounds so soft and feminine. I have to clear my throat.

"For *you*, mostly," he says.

He spears another bit of food and lifts it to my mouth, and even though I can feed myself just fine, I don't have the heart to tell him to stop. The pure look of enjoyment in his eyes, at just the fact he's feeding me…once again I am touched.

It hits me then that he ordered the food even before the medic suggested I was malnourished. Do I look that frail?

The thought makes my head dip to look toward my body, but

Aqnar's finger under my chin stops that movement. He tilts my head toward him as he feeds me another piece, his thumb brushing away a bit of sauce that lingered on my lips.

So I let him feed me, taking the opportunity to watch him as the thoughts in my head go to war—one side fighting to believe this is reality, the other arguing that this is too good to be true.

For the next few minutes, as he feeds me, the air between us thickens. Every lift of the fork as he puts it between my lips, every brush of his thumb against my soft flesh, every breath, every time I catch his gaze, absolutely everything between us seems magnified and multiplied a thousand times.

When he moves his thumb again, brushing away some sauce from my lower lip, it feels like he goes slower than usual, his breath hitching as his thumb makes its way across the plump skin.

His golden eyes darken, and his throat moves. Too small for the fork, he takes the last piece of food in the box between his fingers and brings it toward my lips. I don't even jerk away. My chest is heated, my core almost bursting into flames, and every nerve ending in me waits with anticipation as he slips his fingers into my mouth.

My eyes almost roll back at the contact, and I hear him groan as my mouth closes around the digits. When he pulls them back slowly, my pussy clenches, wanting something to grab hold of like how my lips are grabbing hold of his fingers, and I am both horrified and thrilled by the response.

"Klaok smells something sweet," Klaok breaks the silence and lifts his head from his box of food. "From you," he says, his gaze pointed to my lap.

It takes a moment before horror makes my eyes widen. He can smell my arousal.

My cheeks blaze as I shift on the seat and Aqnar growls low.

"Klaok, take as many boxes of food as you like and go to your room. *Please.*"

Klaok's ears stand up tall, totally unaware of the dangerous hunger that I can see as I stare into Aqnar's eyes.

My heart beats like I'm running a marathon. The look in his eyes is completely primal and full of need.

"Klaok has a room? His very own?"

"Yes," Aqnar almost growls. "This level has many free rooms. Find one, I don't care which one, and go there now."

Klaok bounces up, his thin legs doing a funny dance as he grabs more boxes than I think he can carry and rushes from the room as if he is afraid Aqnar will change his mind.

Now alone, the lump in my throat forces me to swallow hard. All this time, Aqnar has not turned his eyes away from me.

He sets the empty food box down and leans forward from his crouch, forcing me to lean back on the seat. He prowls over me like this until I'm almost flat, with only the cushions behind me supporting my back.

"My *ari...*"

I'm stunned to silence, my eyes widening as I stare up at him.

Seeing my shock, Aqnar closes the distance, his mouth closing over mine. I don't resist, and I realize I've been waiting for this all evening. His tongue delves into my mouth, tickling mine, and my body sings for him immediately.

I groan, rolling my tongue against his own.

It's a kiss that leaves me breathless. One that sends shockwaves of need down to my center. My clit throbs, and my breasts feel like they're suddenly swollen and need freedom. My entire body screams for his touch.

I have never—NEVER—been drawn to a man the way Aqnar draws me.

"You are *mine,*" he says, breaking the kiss for a moment.

I open my mouth to protest, and he closes it with another bruising kiss.

"You don't feel it yet, but I will wait." He breathes against my lips. "I can wait."

My heart thumps and a big part of me aches.

I want this to be true.

For the first time in my life, I'm drawn to a man that makes me feel...worth much more than I have ever felt in all my life.

"I want you to be happy here, Marion," he says. "I want you to be happy with me."

I want him…I want this more than anything I've ever wanted in my life…so why am I so afraid?

"I know it will take time. But Marion…I will wait for eternity if it means I get to have you."

My walls fall down, crumbling into a thousand pieces at those words.

Aqnar reaches for me, his hand raking through my hair to caress the back of my head as his lips press into mine.

His embrace feels like heaven, and as my mouth opens to his, Aqnar releases a low moan.

His tongue dips into my mouth, dripping sweet honey that ignites my soul as I open up to him.

"Aqnar," I murmur. I know even before I say the words that I'm positive it is what I want. "Mark me."

Aqnar freezes. His lips break contact as he lifts his head enough so he can look at me.

"What did you say?"

"Mark me," I whisper again.

Reaching up, I grasp his neck the way that's most natural, with the palm of my hand moving to his nape.

A deep rumble shakes us both as Aqnar's eyes roll back and he releases one of the sexiest groans I have ever heard from a male.

"When you touch me there…" he rumbles.

"What?" I whisper. "What happens when I touch you here?"

"I want to have your sweet, soft body beneath me, my cock buried deep, *deep* inside you."

A lightning strike of something goes straight down to my pussy, making my little bud throb and grow, seeking attention. I yelp, need making me shiver, as Aqnar reaches down with his free hand and cups me entirely.

"Here?" I whisper, feigning ignorance as I rub my palm against his nape again.

Aqnar's eyes roll back once more, and he groans.

"Back on Ockorius, I pushed you away because you touched me there. I would have taken you there and then, Marion. Gods know it is hard not to take you now. But I will wait till you are ready. Till you trust me. Till you understand, I am drawn to you not because I want something, but because you are what I need."

I can't help but throw myself at him, pressing my lips against his in a kiss that quickly turns into our tongues crashing together.

Without thinking, my hand rubs at the nape of his neck again, and he growls into my mouth.

"Marion, it is best you cease. I am already at the limits of my control," Aqnar growls.

As he presses into me, there is a hardness that throbs. One I realize is not his leg as I'd thought.

He's even bigger when hard. I can feel it. And it's only making my core clench, sweet nectar flowing through me. Anticipation builds with just the thought of him piercing me, sinking deep inside me.

I want this.

"Marion..." Aqnar groans, his teeth grit, his face pained. "We should cease. My control..."

"No," I whisper, swallowing the lump of anticipation that's rising in my throat at what I'm about to say. "I want...I want you to lose control. I want you to mark me."

I want this to be real.

Aqnar freezes before bracing on his arms above me, his eyes searching mine even as the gold is slowly diluted by threads of black.

"You do not mean it."

Hell, I'm going to do this, aren't I?

I don't take time to think it over, lest I change my mind...lest the moment passes and this sudden bravery of mine dissipates.

Pulling my arm into the cloak I'm still wearing, I lift it and pull my head through the opening before letting it fall behind me.

I am only left in the garments Aqnar had procured for me. The dark-colored, short-sleeved tunic and box shorts that serve as panties underneath.

Aqnar's gaze slides down my body, taking in all the skin that's visible.

I don't know if it is possible, but his gaze becomes even more heated, and when he locks eyes with me, my breath hitches in my throat.

That predatory darkness in his eyes. The same darkness that tells my mind to run but makes my body weak. I have never seen a man look at me the way Aqnar is looking at me right now.

It's like he wants to devour me.

Like he wants to consume every part of me and make me his.

"Aqnar…" I breathe.

"Tell me no," he says, his voice hoarse with what can only be need. "Tell me no, *at once*, Marion. You are not ready."

Oh, but I am.

His voice, his words…they make me shiver. I'm already soaked because of the tension between us, my skin itching for his touch.

Aqnar watches my every slow movement as I slip my arm into the sleeve of the tunic before lifting it over my head. My naked breasts jiggle, drawing his attention as I fall back against the couch, and his gaze moves down my body, drinking me in.

The tension between us feels like there's electricity in the room, surging in the air.

"Marion…" he groans and only a moment passes before he leans in and his lips crash against mine. He drinks me in. His kiss brutal, *primal*, and filled with raw need.

My whole body lights up like all my nerves come online at once and all I can feel is him. Aqnar.

When he grasps the mound of one breast, squeezing lightly, I moan into his mouth just before Aqnar's lips slip from mine.

He sucks and nibbles on my jaw, going down my chin, my neck, to my collarbone, and my back arches to meet him.

A soft whimper goes through me when his lips close over my breast, sucking on the hard bud as he moans with pleasure.

"Oh my God," I whisper.

Aqnar rumbles something.

"No, not a god," he kisses from my nipple, drifting down to my belly button, "but I intend to treat you like a goddess as long as you will have me."

When his fingers grip the waist of the box shorts, my breath hitches as I look down at him slipping them down my thighs.

But he's purely focused on the center of my thighs, his nose dipping to press against my clit as he inhales deeply.

"By the Gods, female," he growls.

He pulls the box shorts down my legs in one smooth move and growls as he looks at my sex.

Now without the cover of the cloak, the absolute hunger in his gaze is unhidden, and all I can remember is his wet tongue writhing deep in my cunt. There is no thought, no fear. I simply shudder as the reins on my control slip when he grasps the inside of my thighs. With his thumbs, he spreads my inner lips apart, his gaze devouring my heated pink flesh.

A rumble of satisfaction goes through him as he looks at me, making my clit throb and a fresh wave of wetness coat my folds.

"You are the most beautiful thing I have ever laid my eyes on," Aqnar rumbles.

His thumb brushes over my clit and I jerk against him. Those dark eyes flick to my face, and he does it again, watching my reaction.

"Haa," I moan, and Aqnar's eyes drip pure dark need.

"Drip for me, my ari. The scent of your slick is driving me senseless," he murmurs, his voice the deepest rumble, before his tongue slowly swipes through my folds.

A satisfied grumble leaves him as he adjusts himself so he can lap at me, his mouth closing over my pussy as he sucks, murmurs of pleasure vibrating through his chest and driving me insane.

I don't know which is better—the feel of his tongue writhing through my folds or the sounds he's making while he eats me. It's not long before I can't keep still. It's too much. I pant and squirm, the world going dim as my eyes close and my body shudders.

Distantly, I know I'm holding on to the cushion beneath me, gripping it for dear life as Aqnar grasps my hips and forces my cunt down on his face, forcing me to fuck his tongue.

A scream of pleasure leaves my lips as I reach my first peak, and unlike what usually happens when sweet fever crashes through me, it doesn't stop.

My body shakes, my skin taking on a fresh sheen of perspiration at the intensity of my release. And I'll be damned because Aqnar keeps his mouth nestled in my folds.

A groan escapes him as he sucks on my cunt, prolonging the longest orgasm I've ever had in my life.

"Aqnar!" I scream his name, breathless as I gulp in huge breaths of air. My pussy clenches hard on his tongue, but I want more.

I want to feel real hardness.

I want to feel filled.

A growl rumbles from Aqnar as he slows the movements of his tongue, and when it slips from my entrance, he swipes it through my folds in one slow lick, savoring the taste of my juices.

"I need you," I whimper, my body still producing uncontrollable jerking motions.

That feeling of needing to be filled consumes me. I've never wanted something as badly as I want this alien before me and my pussy clenches on nothing as if in agreement.

He shakes his head. "Not here," he says, and I feel an immediate sense of loss.

Reaching for him, I thread my hand through the fibers of his hair.

"Please...I can't wait."

I can tell he hesitates even still and the most delicious thought flashes in my mind. Reaching down between us, I run my index and middle finger slowly through my slick folds, a soft moan leaving my lips at the contact.

"I need you, Aqnar," I breathe.

A shiver goes through him as he watches me lift those same fingers and bring them to my lips. That seems to do it, for Aqnar rises on his knees, his eyes on me as he licks his lips, the sheen on his bronze skin a telltale sign of the pleasure he just incited within me.

He jerks off his vest and when it falls to the floor, my eyes finally get the chance to move down the sculpted muscles in his chest. A shudder goes through me as I look at him.

Those muscles in his chest flex as he works the clasp at his waist, releasing his trou, and when it falls to land at his knees, I can't help but stare at his cock as it bounces forward.

Throbbing and erect, a thin line of precum seeps from its center.

Ridges run from the upper side of the shaft, straight from the base to the slightly flared tip. The thought of him forcing that thing inside me makes me ache with need.

"Marion," Aqnar groans as he grips his base, his gaze falling down my body.

"Yes?" I whisper, unable to pull my gaze from the cock in his hand.

His long lashes fan over his cheeks as his gaze dips. He looks like an intoxicated man with his lids so low.

"You are perfect," he whispers. "You are…so perfect."

I bloom at his words, my skin flushing and my body aching for his touch.

I shift closer, shuffling my bum against the couch to better position myself, and when Aqnar reaches between us, his fingers brushing over my entrance, I arch toward his touch.

"So soft…" he whispers, his fingers brushing over my clit before he dips one to my entrance and slides the digit inside me.

My pussy clenches on it and I moan. But I want more. I *need* more than that, and I can't stand the torture. As he pulls his finger from me and lifts it to his lips to suck on it, I know I am gone.

He will undo me.

"Aqnar…" I breathe, and he rumbles in response as he leans toward me once more until we are face to face.

Our breaths mingle as we stare into each other's eyes before I feel the hardness prod, sliding between my folds. The flared head of his cock presses against my entrance as Aqnar holds my gaze.

"My *ari*," he whispers, before closing the distance, his lips sealing with mine as his cock presses into my core. I gasp into his mouth at the feel of it. It's warm. Oh so warm, and already, it feels so good. As Aqnar clasps the back of my head, supporting my skull in his hand, he cradles it as his lips leave mine and he looks down at me, never breaking our gaze.

It's intense, this feeling. More than anything I have ever felt before.

He eases into me some more, enough for the head of his cock to press past that ring of resistance and pop inside me.

My eyes roll back as we both inhale deeply, his muscles twitching as I grab his arm, and my stomach clenching. Sweet nectar fills my channel at the feel of him inside, already stretching me to my limit. Yet, I want more. I *need* more.

"Marion," he breathes. "You feel too good. So wet and warm and *tight.*"

A moan rumbles from him as he slides deeper, and my head falls back as I wrap my legs around him. As Aqnar slides into me, his head dips and he takes my lips once more, his kiss sweet and languid like his movements, as he gets me used to his length and girth.

My hips spread wide, the walls of my cunt stretched to accommodate this golden god.

His sweet, slow fucking sends me into another world, and I surrender to him.

As his pace picks up, one of his hands finds my clit and a shudder goes through me as I reach an unexpected peak.

"Yesss," he growls, breaking our kiss, before gripping my hips with both hands and seating himself fully within me.

My back arches as I inhale deep, my eyes rolling over.

But Aqnar doesn't let up, and I don't want him to.

I'm in a sort of dream state, my body succumbing to endless jolts of pleasure as I surrender to him.

He pounds into me, going into a frenzy as he too surrenders to the heat between us. And I can only hold on to him and let him fuck me the way I've been wanting him to fuck me for so long. My pussy feels tender and swollen, but not ready to give up the pleasure that's making me drip.

And as he pounds into me, my entire body shudders as if I'm seizing, another orgasm rendering me breathless.

When he finally presses down hard on the cushions, his hips pressing into mine as he forces his cock to my deepest, sweetest point, his body stills as a loud rumble leaves his throat.

The base of his cock jerks, pulsing at my entrance, as his spend shoots deep inside me and I know that after today, I can never let him go.

22

Aqnar

My spend leaks from my mate's tight cunt as I lift her into my arms. Her legs wrap around my waist as she pants, our mating having drawn away all her energy.

Her skin is flushed, and she is warm. I want nothing more than to smear my seed all over her, but that will have to wait because there is another more pressing urge.

My cock throbs even though I've just released streams of spend.

I want more. And I want to mark her. *Now.*

But her sweet, tight little cunt isn't ready for that strain yet. My mate is tired.

Gripping her to me, I head to the lift that will take us to the second level of my home. Marion shifts and moans, her body releasing another shiver as I stand on the platform and it rises.

The lights for the sleeping room come on as soon as I enter. Just like the rest of the place, it is decorated with base furnishings. A basic nest. White sheets made from soft *juuli* feathers cover a bed at the center of the room. I head directly for that and rest my mate gently down.

My cock slips from inside her, coating her legs with spend, and she shivers again, a soft moan escaping her lips. Her chest heaves as she looks at me through lowered lashes, her gaze falling down my frame to land on my hard cock. Bracing upright on her arm, she puts herself into a sitting position before she reaches for me.

I jerk at the contact of her small hand on my shaft.

"Marion…" I warn, but nothing prepares me for the feel of her hot mouth on my tip.

A deep moan bellows from me as I look down to see her pretty little mouth stretching over my girth.

"Marion," I rasp.

She can hardly get her mouth over it, but it's more pliable than the rest of my shaft and she manages to get it in, sending a shockwave of need right through me.

The urge to pull it out of her mouth and spin her on her belly so I can seat myself inside her again almost has me losing focus.

"Mm," she says, unable to speak because her mouth is filled.

What the gods is she doing?

That hot little tongue circles my flared tip before dipping on the more sensitive inside, running all along the edge.

"Marion," I warn, my legs almost going weak when she bobs her head over my tip.

"Marion…"

She pulls the tip from her mouth, panting little hot breaths that are driving me insane.

"You didn't mark me," she says, and her words make me groan.

"I'm trying not to."

She pauses and looks up at me, confusion in her eyes…and a sliver of fear.

"You don't want to?" Her hand slackens on my shaft and I reach for her, closing my fist over hers so she can't let me go.

"Oh, I want to. But the last thing I want to do is hurt you, Marion." My explanation does nothing. That slight fear that showed in her eyes is growing, turning into something else I don't like, and with it is that hardness that I saw once in her eyes and never want to see again.

"You are human," I continue. "Do you even understand what you ask?"

She glances away from me and my stomach clenches.

"I will bite you, Marion," I whisper, reaching for her and threading my hand through her hair. "It will bring you pain."

She turns to look at me. "Bite me? Where?"

My hand wanders down to her neck, my fingers brushing over the soft skin there. I feel her throat move under my fingers.

"I want you to...I don't care about the pain..."

Her words make me bleed with need and I fight for control to prevail.

"Marion..."

"If I am your mate, Aqnar..." Her gaze bores into mine, vulnerability, openness, everything showing in those eyes. "If I am your mate, I want to feel the bond like you do. I want to know I am yours, without a doubt."

"You are mine."

"Then show me."

I jerk as her head dips once more, her pink tongue extending to my tip, swirling against the sensitive skin there. I harden even more underneath her fist, and when she locks eyes with me as she stretches her lips over my tip, I know I can hold on to control no longer.

A growl leaves my lips as I pull away from her. Her eyes widen, shock and confusion flooding them before I grasp her by the hips and flip her.

Pretty little ass in the air, her tight wet cunt glistens with the sheen of our spend. That shock in her eyes quickly changes to need as she twists her head so she can look back at me. Bracing against the bedding, she widens her legs, spreading her thighs even more.

My gaze goes black, need consuming me. Like a male blinded by lust, I reach for her, the flesh of her soft hips supple underneath my palm. And as my tip glides over her entrance, the sweet little moan she utters drives me over the edge.

"Marion..."

Her name is all I can say as I drive into her, my cock seating almost halfway with the first thrust. She cries out to me, her voice thick with need and my fangs descend, ready to do what she begs. Gripping onto her hips, I slide back painfully slowly, the walls of her pussy clenching on to my shaft before I drive forward again, seating myself deep inside my mate.

"Oh fuck!" she screams.

I start slow, fighting against the urge to plow into her, but when she throws her hips back against me, I lose all hope of sanity.

Releasing a growl, I barrel into her, her cries of pleasure a song I will hear for days as she collapses beneath me, no longer able to hold herself up.

"Aqnar!"

"*My ari.*"

I lean over her as she tilts her head back, revealing her neck and I know it is time. I bend to her neck, kissing the soft flesh there before I run my fangs against her skin. She shudders and her pussy grows slicker, wetter, warmer, *needier*.

"*You are mine, Marion,*" I rasp, just before I bite down and puncture her skin.

The sweet copper of her blood runs into my mouth immediately and she screams out, stiffening beneath me.

Her pain makes me want to stop, warring with the urge to complete the bite.

"Don't stop," she pants. "I can bear—ah!"

She cries out again as my fangs go deeper and the essence of my life spirit floods through their tips and into her blood.

Like a desert storm, unpredictable and sudden, my cock stiffens as I reach my peak and spend shoots from my tip, once again filling my mate. She screams into the bedding, her hips writhing, her legs thrashing as her cunt tightens around me, an orgasm catching her unaware.

It is the essence of life spirit. It binds us. Makes us one. And it floods through her system, bringing only pleasure and erasing the pain of the bite.

I don't release her until every drop is inside her. Only then do my fangs retreat.

I grip her hand, pistoning inside her, the wet sound of our mating filling the room as my cock slides deep inside her. She is limp beneath me, her eyes rolled over, only a series of moans leaving her frame as I fuck her.

Closing my mouth over the wound, I run my tongue over the marks my fangs made, sealing them while never stopping my rhythm.

Marion shudders underneath me, as she rises to another peak, her pussy clenching down hard on my cock and sending me over the edge.

Rising, I lift her back with me, never separating us as I settle back on my haunches and fuck her sweet pussy.

She cries out to me, collapsing back as I support her. Lovingly, her hand reaches back and cups my jaw, her eyelids low as she tilts her head back so she can see me. So languid...I've never seen anything more beautiful.

And as I bury myself deep inside her one last time, I bend so I can take her lips in mine.

My mate. My ever-so-sweet mate. She has my mark. She will feel the bond as strongly as I do now. As I hold her, our bodies riding out the bliss consuming us, I know the fates have chosen the best for me.

23

Marion

When I wake, I am alone.

I blink at the white ceilings, gathering my bearings. Nestled in the soft bedding, thoughts of exactly what happened the day before rush through my mind.

There's an ache between my legs, the center of my thighs still moist with release.

Aqnar…

I groan as I lift my hand to my neck and wince a little at the warm flesh there.

Aqnar bit me yesterday, *marked* me, and the memory makes my heart thump hard. The mate bond. He activated it, so it should be there now…right?

I gulp, my heart hammering harder as my fingers continue to brush over the tender spot. It doesn't hurt unless I touch it, and even then, it's just a slight ache, but the presence of that slight pain tells me I didn't dream of the mark. It really happened. Only…nothing else seems to have followed through.

Panic starts to rise deep in my belly as I sit upright, searching through me, searching for…something, *anything*!

I don't know what a mate bond should feel like, but I'm certain I shouldn't feel normal. Aqnar's eyes fucking bled black in his need to mark me. I doubt my eyes would do that, but there should be *something*. Something…different about me.

As I sit in the bed, the seconds ticking by feel like they halt and stagger as realization slowly hits.

The mark is there…but there is no bond.

I can feel that's the truth just as much as I can feel the *nothingness* inside me. The absence of something that *should* be there.

I grip my chest, my fingers digging into my skin as the horror of reality hits me hard.

There is no bond.

The breaths coming hard through my nose rack my chest and I don't think I can calm down.

Aqnar's absence takes on a whole new meaning, and my eyes widen.

Staggering from the bed, the soft bedding parts to reveal my nakedness, and fresh spend runs down my legs.

My pussy clenches and my clit throbs at the sensation and I have to bite back a moan. What we did last night…I'd never EVER had anything like that before. Never before had my body reacted to a man the way it did to Aqnar. The way he made me *feel*.

Some more spend escapes and it makes lust shoot through me, followed right behind by a black hole opening in my belly to swallow me whole.

I'll have to leave. I'm not his mate.

No matter how my body sings for him. No matter how much I want this to be true. I can't stay.

I can't…stay.

The knowledge hits me hard and I kind of jerk-stagger toward the door before I pause.

Where is he, anyway? Did he realize this was a mistake and just decided to leave? Is he out there somewhere trying to figure out how to tell me this has been a big fucking mistake?

That hole inside me grows deeper. How can something that felt as good as it did last night be a mistake?

Guess I fucked around and found out. Literally.

FUCK!

Chest heaving, I glance around the room, my brain ticking, my sanity returning, and with it my sense of survival.

I have to leave before he returns. I can't face him again. Knowing the truth, having my body tell me with no doubt that this isn't real is enough. I don't need to hear him say it too. I don't need to get my heart broken twice.

There's a small corridor down one side of the bedroom and I head that way, sure it must be a bathroom of some kind. And I'm right.

There are no towels or any tissues that I can see, so I turn to what looks like a tap and swipe my hand underneath it. Surprisingly, it turns on, running warm fresh water. I wet my hand and wipe away as much slick as I can get from my legs and then between my folds.

With each brush of my fingers against my sensitive flesh, I jerk. My pussy feels a bit swollen, but each brush of my fingers only reminds me of the night before, and with that comes need.

A sob bursts from my lips as I fight the feeling back and work feverishly to wipe away the evidence of Aqnar's release.

This hurts. *Doing* this hurts. An emotional pain that I wish was physical. At least, if it was physical, I could bandage it and numb it, essentially pushing it away. But this…this is so much worse. Each swipe of my hand feels like I'm wiping him out of my life, and another sob racks my frame.

It's one of those cries that come without tears—my body trying desperately to be strong while my mind becomes frayed.

Finally clean enough, I hurry back to the bedroom. It takes me a while to notice a thin line in one of the walls and when I approach it, it opens, becoming wider to reveal rows of neatly pressed clothes. *His* clothes. There is another ache in my heart, another part of me falling into the black hole.

I stare at the garments, not wanting to touch them, but I have no choice. I have no idea where my clothes are. Squeezing my eyes shut, I grab the first piece my fingers land on. It's a seashell white shirt that will probably look like a dress on me. Gulping, I grab it and slip it on. The thing hangs below my knees and the neckline almost exposes my breasts. Luckily, it has two strings that thread through the plunging neckline. I grab one with my teeth while pulling on the other with my hand. Soon I have them tied and I know I'm ready.

I step out of the room, my heart hammering in my ears like it's making its own death symphony. But apart from my pulse beating in my ears, there is no other sound.

Standing on the lift that will take me down to the lower level, I look around for a way to activate it, but it begins moving on its own. I'm on the lower floor in a matter of seconds and I spot the cloak I'd discarded on the couch. That only brings back more heated memories that I try to push away.

Grabbing the cloak, I slip it over my head. I don't know where my shoes are but there's a pair by the door. They'll just have to fit.

I'm almost outside when I hear a small voice behind me.

"Master is leaving?"

Klaok. Fuck. I forgot about him.

I freeze, not immediately knowing how to respond, but after a few seconds, I decide it's best to just tell him the truth.

"It didn't work, Klaok." I turn to find him standing with his ears flat against his head, his hands clasped and wringing with worry. My heart aches. I was just going to leave without him. But we are together now. I can't just go.

"Master's bond is not true?"

His words make another ache go through me and I shake my head, fighting the tears threatening to grow in my eyes.

"It's not." I swallow hard. "Aqnar marked me last night and…and nothing has changed. I feel the same."

Klaok seems to grow even smaller than normal and my heart aches some more.

"I don't think I can stay here, Klaok." Well, I *know* I can't stay here. Even if Aqnar allows me to stay, which I'm sure he'll offer, I can't. Eventually, he'll find his true mate, and then I will have to leave. It will only hurt more then.

"I have to go."

Moving closer to Klaok, I crouch so I'm on his level and give him a hug.

"Master is leaving Klaok?"

I sniff, his words making a tear slide down my cheek. "I'm sure we'll see each other again," I lie. "And I'm sure Aqnar will take great care of you." And that's no lie. If Aqnar's shown me anything so far, it's that he's a considerate male. I know without a doubt that Klaok is in good hands.

Pulling away from Klaok, I stand and turn back to the door.

"Klaok wishes to come with master."

I take a deep breath, my tongue ready to tell him it isn't the best idea. I don't even know how I will survive once I step out of these doors, much less with another being under my care. I will survive, but it won't be easy.

"Master is Klaok's friend."

I squeeze my eyes tight. This is hard.

As if he knows I'm still going to say no, he continues. "Klaok can help master on the outside. Klaok knows many things." He pauses. "And Klaok does not wish to be alone without Klaok's only friend."

I open my mouth to tell him that, despite all that, it still isn't a great idea to come with me. But the doorbell rings. It's so sudden, I startle and my blood runs cold.

Aqnar.

But when the door doesn't open and my brain comes back online, I realize one fact. The doorbell rang. He wouldn't ring the doorbell to his own home.

With much hesitation, I press the button that opens the door. Immediately, the visitor walks briskly inside. My eyes widen on the person's back.

I can tell she's female…and she's nothing short of gorgeous.

White hair the likes of Aqnar's flows down her back, and her flawless bronze skin is displayed in a white sleeveless dress that reaches her toes. Balancing a box in her hand, she turns and her gaze lands on me. Her mouth falls open in surprise.

"Gods of Atar…he didn't tell me you were *this* beautiful." Without waiting for a greeting, she sets down the package she had in her hand and her gaze falls to Klaok. Her face morphs into more surprise.

"And you must be the newot." She gives Klaok a smile. In response, Klaok steps closer to me.

The movement doesn't make her smile falter and her gaze turns back to me, assessing me with such precision I'm happy I pulled on the cloak. When her eyes fall to where my nub is, the fact there is no second arm holding that part of the cloak up is clear. But her gaze moves past it without skipping a beat.

Her eyebrows rise. "This is most surprising…and most *delightful.*" She grins, displaying perfect teeth.

I glance at Klaok and realize he's moved even closer to me. My heart clenches. I can't leave him. He's like *me*—lost in this new world. And…Aqnar rescued him so he can be my company. We are in this together.

"You must be Marion," the woman says, drawing my attention from my friend who has now retreated so much he's almost hidden in the folds of my cloak.

"Um, yes, I'm Marion anddd…who are you?"

The woman flashes me an even more dazzling smile.

"Oh, where are my manners," she says. "I am Aqnar's one and only womb mate. His sister, Aquila."

His *sister*?

"He told me his mate is here, and I thought it best to introduce myself while he is out. Otherwise, I might not get the chance to for the next few days." She turns her gaze to the upper levels. "Since you will be confined to your sleeping quarters."

I get what she's alluding to almost immediately and my cheeks warm, along with the hole of desolation growing in my gut.

Mate. She thinks I'm his mate.

"I am so very happy to meet you!" she says, rushing toward me and pulling me in for a hug. Shock causes me not to respond, my arm hanging by my side. "We are family now," she says.

Family. A new ache hurts my chest and I need to pull away. Family is not something I had back on New Earth. And it's not something I'll have now. His sister might not know what's happened yet. She doesn't know the mark failed.

Releasing me, she heads for the box she brought and quickly undoes the wrapping.

At first, I can't even see what she pulls out. It looks like a pile of layers upon more layers. When she finally takes it out, I see it's a dress. No, not just any dress. It's one that looks like it's been made for a princess in a fairytale. Layers upon layers of leaf-shaped pink and purple pastel fabric comprise the skirt. The bodice is a thick, almost see-through fabric that looks like it would force my breasts up past my clavicle. All of that, and the dress looks like it's worth a year's wages.

"This is for you," she says, beaming. But my shocked reaction must be obvious because she pouts a little. "You don't like it?"

I have to blink several times to clear my vision as I stare at the thing. "I…"

"Too much?"

I don't…know what to say. I'm still caught between mourning something that never was and needing to escape this horrible reality in which I awoke. My brain can't find sentences to answer her and Aquila's shoulders slump.

"I knew you would think that. That's why I brought this!"

Out comes another dress. One that looks like silk infused with gold. One that would stick to my curves like a second skin if I ever put it on.

"Aqnar said I should bring clothes. He didn't tell me what *type*." She grins, her eyes growing mischievous, and I stare at her, my face expressionless.

"I *did* bring other, more normal *regular* clothes…" she says, winking at me.

She dips into the box again and removes what looks like several dresses and other things, smiling at each as she spreads them on the couch.

"Of course, we'll have to go shopping, get you proper sizes and things you like, but I thought these would work for the time being." She turns to smile at me when her smile suddenly drops. Seeming to see my reaction to all this for the first time, her eyes widen slightly.

"Is something wrong, my brother's dear *ari*?"

The word only makes me ache more.

I clear my throat. "No, nothing's wrong. It's just…"

"Too fast? Too much?" She sets the item in her hand down. "I've been told I can come on too strongly sometimes." She smiles at me, one less brilliant than the others. "I'm just very excited about this new development. I have seven brothers. Aqnar is the first to find a mate. Now I get to have a sister *and* little kits added to our bloodline!"

Babies? Oh, God. We didn't use protection, but my implant should stop any pregnancies. It wasn't removed before I left New Earth and they'd outlawed my breeding, so I should be safe. For now.

"Oh, too much again," she says. "By the gods, I'm making a mess of this," she whispers, more to herself than to me.

I force a smile. "No, it's not you. It's…"

It's then that her eyes narrow slightly, and she finally seems to take me in. Her eyes move to the door behind me, before moving from the too-big shoes she can see jutting from under the cloak, right up to my face.

"You were on your way out?"

I release a breath. Might as well tell her. I can't stay either way.

"I was." I glance around the home. "Do you know where Aqnar is?

She shrugs. "Off doing something. He is often called away by the prince to do some business off-world. But I believe he had to report to the crown offices today. Seeing as he is the only one who has returned, and the prince is still out there. I believe he did not want to wake you from your slumber since he will only be gone for a short while." Her gaze warms, but her eyes narrow some more as she takes me in. "A mate that's not Atari…"

Her head tilts as she gazes at me, and I can see a million thoughts going through her head before her eyes widen and she plops down on the table in front of me.

"Forgiveness of the gods…you must be confused. It's been so long since I found my mate, I've forgotten what the bond does to you. You must be baffled with all the barrage of emotions, the need for release… your body must be burning up and your cunt must be so sore." She glances at my lap, and if everything she just said didn't feel like a lie, I would have balked at how forward she is. "I should have brought soothing salts."

She stands abruptly and heads toward the back of the room where there's a corridor leading somewhere else. "I will order them immediately."

Realizing what's happening, my heart hammers against my chest as I reach my hand out to stop her. "There's no need!"

She pauses, turning to look back at me, confusion slowly filling her gaze. "No need?"

"I'm not...in pain. I feel fine."

I mean, apart from the fact that each thought of Aqnar sends a throb down to my pussy and a simultaneous ache through my heart, I'm fine.

Aquila frowns and approaches me. "You do not *seem* in heat."

"Heat?"

"When I found my mate, I went almost insane with need for him. My breasts became swollen, and my cunt too. I needed his cock so badly, I would claw him for it. My need did not end till he sated me several times over several days." She blinks at me and for a few moments, she does not say anything more. Meanwhile, I can only stare back at her, her unfiltered words ringing in my mind.

"It is not the first time that an Atari has mated with a being not of our kind. But I have never heard of the female not surrendering to the bond."

When I drop my hand but don't say anything, she continues. "No fever? No urge to lock yourself in your living quarters and rut my brother?"

My cheeks warm. "No. I—I mean, yes. I *do* want to do those things..." But it's no different than how it felt before. It's just regular horniness.

"It should be an urge that can't be denied." She takes a step toward me. "I was wondering how he managed to leave his female while she's in heat, but I was too excited to question it. My brother finding a mate means my family line will carry on. Not many families have that luxury nowadays."

Guilt consumes me, and my fingers move to the sensitive flesh where Aqnar bit me last night.

A knowing look passes through her gaze.

"I can see he marked you," she says. "Can you feel the bond? Like a cord that's pulling you to Aqnar? Something you can't resist. You just want your bodies touching at all times?"

I want to say yes. That there's something about Aqnar that pulls me, draws me in, from the first moment I laid eyes on him. But that's just normal attraction. What she's describing is something different. And even though I wish I could pretend, deep down I know it.

She must see the look on my face because sadness befalls hers. "Oh dear…"

I stand looking at her, knowing everything she doesn't say. Knowing all the questions she's currently asking but not saying out loud. Knowing they are the same questions I have asked myself. And knowing everything I was considering before is true.

This isn't real.

I'm not his mate, just someone he's attracted to. In the same way I'm attracted to him.

"But…" she mutters, confusion flooding her gaze.

I feel Klaok grip onto my leg and I know I have to be strong for us both.

"He marked me…but I am not his mate." The words feel like lead on my tongue.

Aquila gasps, her eyes going wide, her hands flying to cover her mouth.

"That's impossible," she whispers, but when I don't suddenly laugh out loud and tell her I'm joking, she staggers back to the couch, falling into it. Her head falls into her hands. "I have never heard of this." She looks up at me. "Are you positive you can't feel the bond? Even non-Atari feel the bond immediately. I don't know of any species we have bonded with that haven't felt the bond straight away. It…it's unheard of." She slowly shakes her head, her vision zoning out. "I haven't read of a single case in the archives like this."

Great. So, I'm an anomaly on my home world and on this one too. I almost scoff.

"You were leaving because Aqnar does not know," she whispers, her gaze focusing on me.

I feel the need to protect myself but there is no accusation in her eyes. Just understanding.

"I think he already knows," I whisper.

She shakes her head. "I spoke to him not long ago, before I arrived. I do not think he realizes yet."

That only makes my heart ache even more. Now I can't just run away from my problems. But the thought of facing him, of telling him this isn't real, no matter how sure he thought he was, that feels even worse.

"I can't stay here," I tell her, and to my surprise, she nods.

"I understand. As a female who has been marked and who has a mate, I cannot imagine how you feel. I would not want to face my mate if the bond turned out to be a failure."

A lump forms in my throat as she stands slowly, her sad gaze falling to the wonderful dresses she brought me and I see her excitement, her hope, all fade away.

I've not only destroyed my dreams and Aqnar's but I'm destroying hers and Klaok's as well.

When Aqnar rescued me, I felt like the luckiest woman alive. Now I feel like a blotch, an error.

"I will help you."

Aquila's words pass by my ears and take a moment to register.

"What?"

"I'll help you," she repeats. "I am aware of the circumstances. I am aware you have no one and my brother, even without the bond, will be livid if I leave you on your own." She pauses and takes a deep breath. "He will be livid when he returns, but I will help you. It may be best this way."

I swallow that lump in my throat and nod. Klaok glances up at me, a question in his eyes, but somehow, I trust Aquila. Just like I trust her brother.

Things will work out fine, even if my heart is broken and in tatters.

24

Aqnar

I hurry home as soon as I can.

I've been gone for a few hours and although my home is safe, as are most places on Atar, the thought of leaving Marion alone for an extended time makes my life-organ ache, especially after what happened the last time I left her alone.

I just want to be close to her, and after tasting the sweet nectar that she produces from that tight little slit, that feeling has only increased tenfold. Just the memory of her cream makes me go hard, my cock pressing into my trou.

Taking the steps two at a time as I descend from the landing pad down into my residence, my life organ thrums with anticipation of seeing her again. This day, I will reapply her bandages and help her with another bath. I cannot wait to put my hands on her again and even my fangs begin to drip at the thought of tending to her.

But when I open the door and step into the residence, a chill goes down my spine.

It was only Marion and Klaok who I left here. Only two, so they will not make much noise, but the deadly stillness of the air...the quiet...it makes every warrior instinct in me stand on end.

"Marion?"

My voice echoes in the room as if to tell me that I am alone. Another chill goes through me, and I rush to the lift, standing on the platform as it rises to the upper level.

I know she's not in the room even before I get there.

The bed is made, the covers set perfectly as if no one slept in it the night before. Even the box with the clothes I ordered and had Aquila deliver is sitting there, its lid closed, as if the contents were not removed. My life organ cracks, telling me to turn away, but I drag my feet in, my eyes on the box.

Using one hand, I open it to see the clothes neatly folded inside. Not once piece disturbed. There is a note there too. One written in unique scrawls in a language I do not know.

Activating the device behind my ear, I scan the letters and they soon translate.

Aqnar,

I am sorry.

First, I want to thank you for all you have done for me. I am indebted to you, and I am committed to paying you back for every credit you spent getting me out of that bad situation.

Spending time with you these past few days has been...a once in a lifetime experience. For the first time, I felt like a princess.

Thank you for giving me that.

Your sister has been of help as well. Please tell her thanks and...please don't be angry at her. You may not believe it, but I think she's just looking out for your best interest.

I wish I had someone to look out for me like that.

. . .

You have been the perfect everything. Everything a girl could dream for. And one day, you will also be the perfect mate for someone.

I am sorry this hasn't worked out for us. ~~I really~~ I wished it did. But spending even a few days with you is a time I will cherish forever.

It was nice meeting you Aqnar of Atar.

Your friend,
   Marion

Staring at the paper, it trembles in my hand as I become consumed by rage. Dropping it on the bed, I turn and shout down to the lower level.

"Klaok!"

But there is no response.

I feel another part of my life organ crack. Another fissure that pulls me closer to collapse.

Launching myself over the protective railing, I don't bother waiting for the lift as I jump to the lower level. I land on my feet as I rush to the communicator on the wall.

My womb mate picks up the line after a single ring.

"Aqnar?"

"AQUILA!" I can tell by the sharp gasp that she's gone pale. "**What have you done**?!"

"Aqnar! Is that how you greet your lovely sister who you haven't had a proper conversation with for so long? Even after she traveled to your residence just to bring your female new garments?"

I growl, my rage not making me think straight.

"What did you do to Marion?"

There is a pause and when Aquila says nothing, I punch the wall beside the communicator. "Tell me!"

"I—I did nothing to Marion, Aqnar. I visited. She was there..." She pauses. "And...we thought it best she wasn't there when you returned. It was easier for her that way, I believe."

*"**What**?"*

"You didn't tell me your mate wasn't Atari. I assumed—" When my growl cuts her off, I hear her sob. "I'm so sorry Aqnar. I wanted it as much as you did. But the fates must have been mistaken."

She's talking nonsense. Not making any sliver of sense.

*"**What do you mean**?"* I growl. *"My mate is not here."*

There's a pause and I wish I could see her face. I hadn't thought to do a vid call. I was in a rush.

"You don't realize yet, do you..."

"Realize *what*?"

"The bond Aqnar...there is no bond."

Time stills and I stare at the white wall before me. My heart stutters and I can't breathe.

"Wrong," I utter. I can feel the bond inside me. I know with everything in me that Marion is my mate. Weak, as it is just starting to solidify, but it is there.

"Aqnar..."

"You are wrong, Aquila." My patience is growing thin. Marion knows no one on this planet. Only me. And now she's gone. "You have put such thoughts in Marion's head and now—"

"I didn't! She realized it all on her own. She was about to leave when I arrived!" She sobs and a part of me cringes knowing I'm bringing sorrow to not only my female, but my womb mate as well. "Aqnar, she can't feel the bond. It doesn't exist within her."

The world grows cold around me, and I force myself to breathe.

"What?"

"She doesn't feel the bond. You even marked her, that's the way it begins with most non-Atari, but nothing has changed for the human. She...her body has not responded to the mark. There is no bond."

My fist presses into the wall. "That can't be true. I feel the bond."

Aquila sniffs. "Maybe what you feel is something else. *Need* maybe?"

"Atari do not have the urge to mark those who are not their mates," I growl, trying to make sense of what she is saying.

"I am aware, my brother. I have checked the archives since returning home. I have not come across any pair bondings like yours, neither have I come across any reports of a female being marked that isn't a mate."

I breathe hard, calming myself as her words flow into my mind. Marion is my mate. And I need her with me.

"Where is she?"

"Aqnar, you're not listening."

"Where is she?!"

I need her. I need her with me.

I will not stop till she's by my side. In my bed. Underneath me.

"I can feel the bond. This isn't *need*. It is weak now, but it will grow. I know it."

"Aqnar—"

"I know it! I just need her here. Now tell me, Aquila…where have you taken my mate?"

"And if she's not?"

My growl is her only answer and I hear when she sniffles and takes a breath.

"Well…"

"Tell me, Aquila!"

"Fine!" She sniffs. "She was asking about refugees and homeless shelters, jobs, travel, stuff like that…"

There is a pregnant silence as my eyes widen. *"And you told her about all these things?"*

"Well, yes. Of course, I told her. She might not be your mate, but she is a female in need. I couldn't just let her go off on her own!"

Without waiting to end the call, I hurry from the room. I already know Marion's not on the outside on the grounds of the residence. I would have gotten a notification on the ship that someone was on my property.

As I reach the landing pad, every cell in my body tightens and constricts.

She's out there. Alone.

Marion left me.

I'd thought…I'd thought what we shared last night had been evidence of her growing need. I thought the moment I marked her, the moment my life spirit flooded her veins, that she was mine forever.

I was mistaken.

But I'm not going to let her just walk out of my life. The time for that has passed anyway. I am hers and she is mine.

She's the other part of me and I'd rather die than live without her.

25

Marion

I collapse against the seat of the shuttle, Klaok by my side.

I don't know how I've gotten this far. How I've managed to go through all the officials, the checkpoints, everything, to even get on the shuttle headed to the refugee station called Glycon One Nine. But now that I'm here, seated among many other non-Atari males who are leaving the surface, I relax a little.

There are no other females on board, but I know I am safe. Under Atari law, I should be safe, as long as I keep wearing the bracelet Aquila so kindly gave me.

And she was more than kind. She didn't have to help me at all. She owes me nothing.

I know she only helped me because of her brother, but a part of me wants to think she also helped me because she realized just how shitty my situation is. To be marked but not mated. It had to be the worst thing that can happen to her kind. I feel the weight of it and I'm not even Atari. The last thing I'd want to do is bring shame to Aqnar or his bloodline. He deserves happiness.

A niggling thought whispers to me that he deserves *better*...but I push that thought away.

Despite everything, I know that if I had been proven his mate, I would have given him everything I could offer. I would have loved him to no end. I would have treasured him, for he is priceless.

My heart aches at the thought, and I force myself to sit up straight and keep my face expressionless. These males sitting around me may not bother me because of the bracelet I'm wearing, but I will not make my situation worse by crying in front of them and appearing weak and lonely.

I'm still alive and I will survive on my own. I'll find a way. Like I always have. There will be a lot of time to cry later...a *lot* of time. Years that will feel like eons.

Once again, my heart mourns what it never had. A male that was not mine to claim. A male I shouldn't want as badly as I do.

A part of me wished I was Atari. That there was definitely a mate out there for me somewhere. But I'm only human. Mate bonds don't exist among my kind.

I can only dream.

Settling back, I wait for the shuttle to lift off, and I close my eyes. As the engines come online and the whole cabin hums, I grip the seat beneath me and feel as Klaok grips on to my cloak. I keep my eyes closed, forcing my thoughts away and just listening to the deep hum of the engine. And when the weight shifts and I know we're airborne, my heart clenches again.

Something inside me breaks.

This is it.

This is forever.

As the shuttle leaves Atar, I keep my eyes closed and I don't open them, even when it goes hyper speed and I know we've just made a jump. The only time I open them is when a recording airs through the cabin, stating that we have arrived on Glycon One Nine.

Why I chose this specific station, I don't know. There had been several to choose from, all protected by the crown of Atar.

I know it's probably foolish even heading to a refugee station protected by the very place I'm running from, but I know it won't matter. Aqnar won't come for me. Not when he realizes there is no bond.

He will feel both shame and trepidation at the thought of facing me. And that's just fine.

It's better we never see each other again.

As we disembark from the shuttle and I set foot on this new world, I immediately hate it. It's nothing like the foggy skies and dark roads like Lower Earth, but I can tell by the being's faces that their lives have been hard. It's enough to remind me where I've come from. Who knows, I might fit in well here.

I grip the card and information Aquila gave me and head in the direction of the large building rising off the docks. The registration hall.

Time to start my new life.

It takes just a few minutes to walk from the shuttle to the hall and the whole time, I have to push forward, fighting my legs to keep going. Once I enter the hall, it gets easier.

The alien at the counter barely glances at me before inputting information in the information deck before her.

"Name," she asks.

"Marion," I answer. "But I would like—"

"You would like for it to be kept confidential," the clerk cuts me off. "Yes, yes, I know. You are a female after all. And you?" She glances down at Klaok.

"I am master's friend."

The clerk looks away from him with disinterest. "And friend."

She pulls a transparent card from a pile and stretches it to me. "Job postings can be found here and on the digiforum." She taps on the card. "Your new address is also here. We bid you good beginnings."

I stare at her, and she blinks at me.

"That's it?"

Her bored gaze doesn't move. "Registration is complete."

My eyebrows move up an inch and I offer her a slight smile before taking the card and hurrying from the line. Just as she said, an address, or rather, a small map is displayed on the card. I follow it with Klaok in tow.

Glycon One Nine is big. I can tell already just from walking from the port and into the city. The streets are busy, throngs of beings going to and fro. I fall in line, following the map while keeping aware of Klaok by my side.

Twice we go down the wrong road, but the map adjusts until the blinking circle stops at a huge building before us.

"Guess this is it," I smile down at Klaok. He returns my smile almost nervously.

I can do this, I tell myself as my gaze moves up the large tower before me. So high, the back of my head hits my shoulders, and I still can't see the top of it.

I take a deep breath. I can't believe how easy it was to get housing. It turns out Atar doesn't make it hard for female refugees to get housing and jobs on any of the stations they manage, as long as they are genetically compatible with the Atari race.

That fact hurts, since I'm technically not compatible with the one Atari I want, but it is still a perk of being a human. I'll take it till I can do better.

"Here we are," I say to Klaok. There's a heavy block of weight in my chest. One that's weighing me down. One that's bringing me close to tears. But I tell myself Aquila was right. That this is the right thing, for Aqnar and me.

Squeezing Klaok's hand, I step toward the tower's large doors, and they open automatically.

The person at the reception desk is humanoid but not Atari. She looks similar to a standard human except she has elf ears and two small antennae that branch off the top of them.

"Hello," she greets me, and I hesitate before pushing myself forward.

"Hi, I'm—"

"Marion Hemmings of Earth." She glances at a holo screen in front of her. "Don't worry. The registration block sent your details over."

"Oh?"

"Come this way. I will take you to your room and also provide you with your job information packet." Her smile is dazzling, and I force one of my own.

Following behind her, my eyes roam the expansive corridor that leads to the lift. It looks much like the same type of lift that's in Aqnar's home, except that a protective bar appears as soon as we stand on it.

"You are on level 5," she says, still smiling at me. "Room 5B."

My shoulders stiffen. "Did you say room 5B?"

The universe is playing tricks on me, because that was my room number when I boarded that cursed ship that got me in this situation in the first place.

"No, Room 5T," she says.

My shoulders slump, tension leaving my muscles.

It doesn't take us long to get there, but even as we walk, I can't notice the sights around me. At another time, I would have been amazed by the fact that the corridor is so tastefully decorated with beautiful flowers, their scents and smells filling the hall. Or even the fact that all the women that pass us on our way to my room are well-dressed and seemingly happy. Or the biggest one—the fact that this is nothing like Lower Earth, my home.

All I can think about is the feel of Aqnar's beating heart as I lay against his chest. The way he held me while we slept. And the way his musk filled my nostrils and made me have to squeeze my thighs together to hide my arousal.

When the woman opens the door to 5T, I walk in murmuring thank you as she enters behind me. She's saying something but my mind's not listening, my thoughts still on Aqnar.

When the prerecorded video begins to play from a large screen and she smiles and leaves, I finally figure out that she'd been explaining that she's putting on the job packet.

I flop down on the bed, mildly taking in that this room is like a 5-star hotel room on Lower Earth, and stare at the video playing.

This is the right decision, isn't it? Leaving him? Then why do I feel so...sad?

26

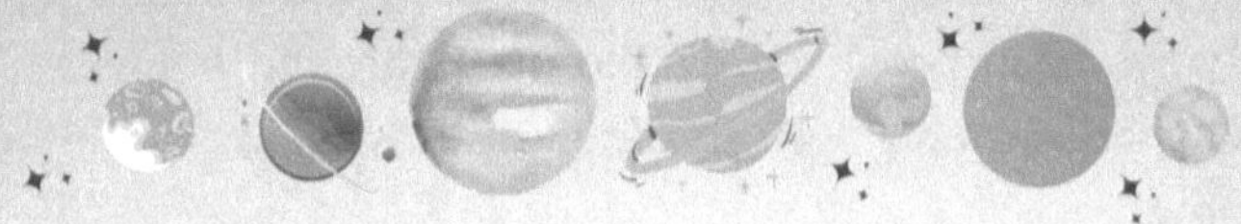

Aqnar

Three days.

It has been three days since Marion left, and I am slowly falling into insanity.

I have searched every station close to Atar and come up with nothing. But she couldn't have gone far. Not so quickly.

My chest burns at the thought of her, the bond aching.

For the hundredth time, I check the logs of my residence to see if she has returned there. But she has not.

Aquila was right. Marion does not feel the bond, or she would have returned. She would not be able to deny its call.

The thought makes my life-organ wring in distress.

I need my mate. I need her warmth. Her smiles. Her presence. If even to be in her presence while the rut consumes me, I would gladly take that pain over this.

Even though I have tried many times to no avail, I reach out through the bond that should be there. That invisible cord that links me to my mate. To Marion.

But it is like the end of the cord reaches out to nothing. As if it is frayed. Broken.

A strong urge fills me, making my life organ swell.

I need to find her.

As I maneuver my ship to what feels like the thousandth station, I stare at the atmosphere as my ship descends.

I need to find her.

Aquila had no information about where Marion had gone. She'd left her to choose. Left her *alone.* Unaware of the dangers out there, having always been protected by the males around her, Aquila does not know what Marion's been through…and what she could be going through now.

I grip my chest, my life-organ stuttering, and I try to pull my mind away from that. I saw Marion fight. Saw the fire in her eyes when the velushan tried to take her away. I have to believe she is fighting now—even if she is fighting to get away from me.

A ping sounds in the ship and I startle, pulling up the notification on my screen as I let the AI take the controls.

A growl leaves my lips.

Another anonymous payment to my account. The amount is so small, when it happened the first time, I thought it was a mistake. But here it is again. This is the second day I have received the same amount and at the same time as the last.

I don't want to even think it, but a part of me knows where the funds are coming from. Or rather, *who.*

I am committed to paying you back for every credit you spent getting me out of that bad situation.

It has to be her. Once again, I try tracing the source of the funds. But she's encrypted it. I almost smile. She's smart.

But I will find her anyway.

The journey to the surface is quick and as my shuttle docks, I am almost out the door before the engine stops humming.

"An Atari warrior?" The dock hand rushes up to me. "To what do we owe this visit?"

A snarl leaves my lips and he pales.

I am in no mood for mindless talk.

Slipping the cloak over my shoulders, I throw him a credit to keep watch on my shuttle till I return. I haven't parked in the designated spots for long visits. I am only here to find my mate and then leave.

I take the main steps heading down to the streets two by two, my gaze scanning each and every passerby.

There is nowhere to head to, and yet, I have to check everywhere. I'd contacted every refugee station near Atar, but none have any record of Marion or Klaok. Either they went somewhere else—which I shudder to think about—or they also kept their identities hidden from the records.

The only way I could get that released is through the crown, and Da'red is still off-world. I'd hate to have to ask his ill father or anyone else for such a favor. I still have not had time to enjoy my mate, much less to have her paraded before others.

But if it comes to that...I will have to do it.

As I walk down the streets, there is a faint ache in my chest. One that wasn't there before. I ignore it. I have not eaten or slept since Marion left. My body will want to collapse soon, but I will not let it.

I must go on.

The streets here are large, yet still they are filled with beings from across the galaxies, the majority of them with similar characteristics as Atari. I scan each of their faces, none of them the one I want to see.

I will head to the major employment establishments first. Ask around. The records may be hidden, but few managers will deny the request of an Atari warrior—especially one made in person. I am prepared to *convince* them to speak using any means necessary. It is the reason I wore my leathers, so they will know my rank. A perk of being on the battlefield for years, fighting for my planet. Fighting so when I finally found my mate, she would have somewhere safe to live.

As I pass one of the towers that house the refugees, the pain in my chest increases. I continue ignoring it, putting one leg in front of the other as I head down the street. There is no use stopping by the tower.

The female who runs it will not give details of the residents. For protection. It is one thing to know where a female works. Another to know exactly which room she resides in. So I push on.

But the pain increases. Every step I take becomes harder, more difficult, until I begin to see dark spots in my vision. Whatever this is, it must go away. I do not have time—

I stagger, bumping into a passerby. Their mild exclamation dies on their lips as my world tilts. I'm aware people are crowding around me. Voices. Shapes. But I can make out none, my mind unable to grasp their words, even their faces.

"Aqnar?"

My lips twist into a smile, one I can barely manage, as I chuckle.

Even in this state, I am hearing her voice.

"OhmyGod! It *is* you!"

Out of all the faces, Marion appears. In this dream, she is even more beautiful than before.

"Let me through! I know him. He is my—"

The crowd parts and she is by my side, her face filled with worry.

I frown when her fingers clasp my cheek, water filling her wide eyes.

"Klaok thinks master is ill."

I frown some more. I would have dreamed Marion, but not the little newot. His annoying voice is not one I want to hear. I only want to hear hers. I want Marion to speak again.

"We have to help him. Aqnar? Aqnar!" She grips my chin and shakes my head. A lazy smile twists my lips.

I would have had her lips on mine if this was a dream… So this is not a dream. It really is her?

"Marion?"

A tearless sob leaves her lips. "Please, can someone help us? I live right here, if you could just help—"

Her voice cuts off as I struggle to my feet. My vision wanes in and out but I manage to stand. She is against my chest immediately, gripping unto my leathers, eyes big and wide.

"Take it easy! What the hell happened to you?"

"So it *is* you," I whisper.

She pales. "You came here looking for me?"

As my head lolls, her eyes grow wider. I do not know how she does it, supporting me as we walk-stagger into the building, but soon we are on the lift and then she and Klaok are helping me into a room.

Marion untangles herself from underneath my arm and pushes me gently, so I fall on what I believe is her bed.

Her hand rakes through her hair and she paces, speaking a million words a minute as Klaok rushes around. I don't know what she says. I don't care.

All I can do is look at her.

I have found her.

I have found my mate.

27

Marion

He is here.

Don't ask me how he did it because I would love to know, but he has found me.

I'd been so careful…but a part of me never thought he would come looking. By the second day, I'd buried all lingering hope and delved into the new job I found cleaning out a nearby bar. I'd even sent two payments back to him, half of the pay I received both times. The refugee station has free housing and meals, so it's not like I was starving or anything. I reckoned I'd better start paying him back quickly because I owed him a shit-ton.

But now…he is here.

What the fuck?

I glance at him on the bed and almost startle. I thought he was unconscious, but there, underneath his low lashes, those golden eyes I'd fallen in love with track my every move.

There is a chime at the door, and I rush away from facing this Atari god to open it.

I don't want to face this. I don't know *how* to face this.

"You called for medical assistance?" the humanoid female at the door smiles at me. She looks just like the clerk on the first floor, and I nod, recognizing that she must work here.

"Yes, he's, he's just inside."

She gives me a small nod and enters the room as I step to the side. I see the moment she spots Aqnar because her steps halt. Seeing him now, from her perspective, and I understand why.

He's huge. My little single bed looks like a child's bed underneath him. Even in his state, he looks strong and virile, like he could pop us both in two in his sleep.

My heart hammers against my chest just looking at him. Did I really have sex with him? Did I really let him pin me down and ram into me from behind?

Even the thought of it now wakes up something inside me that I've been fighting to ignore these past three days.

"What happened to him?" the medic asks.

I shake my head. "I don't know. I found him on the street."

Gathering her bearings, she moves over to the bed and takes out her instruments. As soon as she lifts what looks like a flat stick with an LED light underneath it, bringing it over Aqnar's chest, his hand flies up and grabs her wrist. We, both me and the medic, gasp.

"Leave us," he says.

The medic stutters. "You are hurt," she says. "Y-you are Atari. I am bound to ensure your health. Please let me perform my duties."

"I am fine. Only one thing ails me, and I know how to fix that." Aqnar's eyes find me, and I swallow hard, suddenly wanting to run away again but having nowhere to go. I brought him to my room! Instead, I fist the standard work garments they provided me—a gray blouse with matching gray pants—and wait.

The medic glances at me for help and I nod at her. With a sigh, she puts her instruments back.

"Please—" she begins.

"I will make a note that I sent you away of my own accord," Aqnar says.

The female nods again and smiles, rushing toward the door as if she can't exit soon enough. I watch her go, watch the door close behind her, and I keep looking at it, as if it will erase the male lying on my bed the next time I turn around.

That doesn't happen.

"Marion…"

My breath hitches and I squeeze my eyes tight.

This shouldn't be this hard. It's been three days. Three long days. Three sleepless nights. Three days of pining over the very man that's now in my room. Lying on my bed!

"Marion…*my ari*…look at me."

That ache in my chest feels like it clenches my aorta and doubles down in pressure.

"Aqnar…" I breathe, refusing to turn around. But when I feel the heat of his skin against my arm, I stiffen and can't move.

"Marion…look at me."

I gulp and turn slowly, mildly surprised at how close he is. I didn't hear him move.

"Aqnar, I—"

I don't get to finish my sentence as my chin is grasped and Aqnar's mouth comes crashing against mine.

My legs go weak, and he somehow realizes and catches me as my knees bend.

We shouldn't be doing this. We shouldn't—

But I'm weak against my own urges. I can't stop. He tastes so good, I want more. Even as a sob rises in my chest, I kiss him back.

Aqnar lifts me and turns, bringing me to the bed and he sets me down, his lips still joined with mine. There's a hunger in his kiss. A need that feels stronger than before. He growls my name against my lips and my entire body sings, my skin becoming feverish, my whole being tingling.

It's not fair. How can I say goodbye when I want him like this?

"Why did you leave? I have searched…I have searched so long for you." He breaks the kiss and moves his lips down my neck, his tongue flicking over the scar of his bite.

My thoughts stagger. But when he kisses that spot, sanity returns.

"Aqnar, you shouldn't be here."

"I shouldn't be anywhere else," he growls.

He lifts his head then and looks at me, his eyes completely black. I've seen that before and just like the first time, when I know I should run but couldn't, I am held frozen by the intensity of his dark gaze.

"You are my mate. I almost lost you three times. Don't make me experience losing you again."

"I—"

"*You are mine*," he stares down at me and I finally notice that he has pressed my wrist into the bedding below us, holding me captive.

Everything he is saying is what I want to hear, but none of it is the truth.

"Mine to kiss. Mine to hold. Mine to love."

I shake my head, tears brimming at my eyelids.

"*Mine*, Marion."

How can he say these things knowing the truth? It's only making that pain in my heart grow stronger. A pain I've fought to keep at bay for the last three days.

"Stop," I whimper, the tears finally falling down my cheek. "Just… stop. Is that why you've come here? To make me suffer? You know what you say isn't true."

I blink through the blur my tears have caused. "You know I'm not your mate. Why…why do you insist when the truth is obvious?"

His fingers slacken on my wrist and when I can see him clearly again, I notice the darkness is seeping from his eyes. Soon his golden gaze looks down at me.

"There is no bond," I whisper, pulling my eyes away from him. It hurts too bad even looking at him. How…how in such a short time, did I fall so hard for this male?

"If there was a bond," I continue, "we'd both feel it."

He doesn't answer and I know he knows what I say is true.

When I shift underneath him, he allows me to wriggle from his grasp and I shuffle until I am off the bed. I can't face him, so I keep my back turned.

"You shouldn't have come here," I whisper. "It's only going to make this harder."

"At this rate, my dear human, I am never letting you out of my sight again. You belong to the Atari."

I turn on him, my sorrow, my pain all burning into rage. For that is an emotion I can feel just fine. The other two rip me apart and leave me in shreds. But rage…rage gives me strength.

"I don't belong to *anyone*."

The moment I say the words is the moment I know I made a mistake. His eyes bleed to black almost instantaneously.

"Wrong," he says. "*You belong to me.*"

He moves so quickly, I don't have time to run. Aqnar launches himself across the bed and comes within inches of grabbing me. I scream and my legs finally move. Fear creeps up my spine, followed by something wholly unholy, as I screech and run toward the door.

I'm very aware that this big alien could have grabbed me as I made my way past the bed, but somehow he doesn't, and I reach the door.

Once look back, I know why. Aqnar watches me as I grab the door handle, as if he is daring me to open it and run. Those eyes and the way he turns so slowly, watching my every movement, noting my every breath…he is a predator…and I am the prey.

"*Marion…*"

His voice has changed. It is deeper. Darker. And it sends chills right through me. Good chills. Chills that shouldn't be there. They run down my spine and coalesce in my center.

He shifts on his feet and, affected by whatever instinct there is within me to run and preserve myself, I don't think, I just move.

I'm dashing down the hallway as fast as my legs can take me. Running where? I don't know. A little part of me knows he will catch me, regardless if I make it out of the building or not, but I can't stop myself from running. It's a fear response, and when I hear him behind me, I let out another screech as I head for the lift.

I'm going to make it, I'm going to—

One glance behind me and I yelp, a shock of anticipation shooting through me as I realize just how close he is. He was *letting* me run. No way I'd have made it to the lift, even though it's right in front of me. In the next second, I'm swept off my feet.

He pins me against the wall, and I am mildly aware that other residents have opened their doors to see what the commotion is.

"Go back inside," Aqnar growls so low, I don't know how they hear him, but they all simultaneously close their doors, and we are once again alone.

"Aqnar, this is—"

"This is right." His lips close over mine once more and I am suddenly too weak to fight, to run, to deny this for much longer. So I stop fighting. I lean into the weakness I have for this Atari warrior and wrap my legs around his waist, my hand moving up to tangle in his hair.

"Mm," Aqnar moans into my mouth and I open up to him. Our tongues clash and roll, sucking, slithering, dancing with each other.

It is almost too much. Too much! I feel like I'm floating in a whole new world far from this one.

"I will mark you again," he breaks away and whispers against my lips in between nibbling on them. "I will do anything it takes."

I pant against his lips, relishing in the taste of him. "No. You can't."

"I will do anything, Marion."

"Not that. What's done is done."

"Then we will go away somewhere far. We don't have to live on Atar."

I pause then, pulling my lips from his so I can look into his eyes. A tear runs down my cheek and he wipes it away.

"I could never do that to you," I whisper. "You deserve a mate. A true mate. A good one."

"You are my—"

"But I'm not, Aqnar!"

He only stares at me, his chest heaving as his gaze bleeds from black to gold to black again.

I swallow hard.

Even with those words I uttered, the hardness I feel poking at the curve of my ass, right beneath my center, doesn't die. The thought thrills me. That even in this critical moment, he's still hard for me. It is a selfish thought, but one I can't help but relish in.

"You are my mate," he says. "I claim you here. I claim you now. For anyone seeing, and anyone hearing, Marion Hemmings of Earth, *you are mine.*"

For a split second, I wonder how he found out my surname. I don't remember telling him that…but then a sharp pain in my lower abdomen makes my belly cave.

I stare at him, not understanding what just happened, when the pain comes again, harder this time.

I crumple, my body going inward. Only Aqnar holding me up, forcing my body upright, keeps me from doubling over.

"Marion?" The black in his eyes disappears almost instantly. "Something's happening. What's happening?"

"I…I don't know."

The pain comes again, so hard that I cry out.

It feels like something is carving its way out of my womb. This is different from period cramps, it's much worse, and my mind flies to the worst possible scenario. I'm dying.

But I can't be dying. I was healthy just a few seconds ago.

When the pain comes once more, it's so strong that I see stars.

"Aqnar!" I grip on to him, fear leeching into my voice.

"Marion!"

My vision wanes and when the pain comes one more time, my chest heaves with it, trying to expel everything from my stomach. It fails and nothing comes up, but that doesn't stop my body from trying again.

"What's happening?" I ask, even though I have no clue and I'm pretty sure Aqnar doesn't either.

He grips me, lifts, and begins moving. I don't even know where, only that he's moving very quickly, my name a constant whisper in his mouth.

"Stay with me, Marion."

28

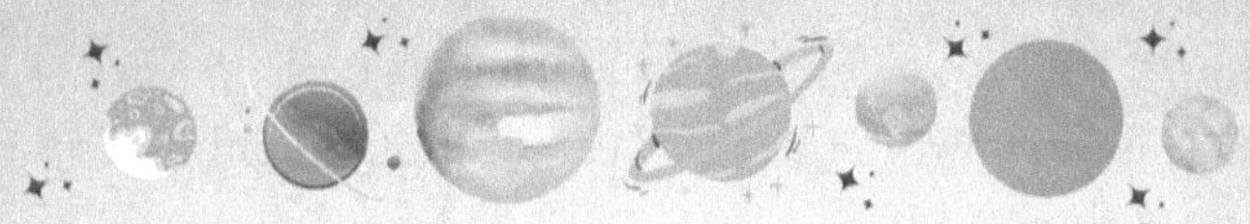

Aqnar

I pace outside of the med bay, time ticking too slowly. My life organ thumps so hard, I think it may escape my chest.

I almost lost her once, twice, thrice, and now four times! How many times will the fates test me?

Leaning on the wall in the narrow corridor, I place my forehead against it, images of my mate's cry, of her pain as I rushed through the tower toward the med bay ring in my ears.

Even when her wounds were raw, I did not hear her cry like that… and that fact is making me think the worst.

But Marion is stronger than she looks. She is a fighter.

Still, the wait is killing me.

I have waited for what feels like ages to get word back. Nothing. It does not spell well. But, at least, I have not yet heard any bad news. I hold on to that fact and I wait. I wait for them to open the doors and tell me my mate will be fine.

But patience is not an Atari virtue. I turn toward the doors, fully intent on demanding they let me see Marion, when I stagger to a stop.

There…deep inside me…I feel something bloom and expand. It hits me so hard, I have to catch my breath. My eyes widen as I pause, making sure I'm feeling exactly what I'm feeling.

The bond…

The bond is…*blooming*.

Gripping my chest, I stare at the door, just as I feel the steady heartbeat of my mate pulsing through the bond.

I reach for it, reaching through that invisible cord that connects us, and I no longer feel a frayed end. Instead, I follow an unbroken path, and I feel *her*.

"Marion?" I whisper, unable to believe it. Before, when I felt the undeniable pull toward her, it had been nothing like this. This…this is tenfold…no, a thousandfold.

The doors suddenly swing open, revealing the antiseptic room, and I stare at the female resting on the floating bed in the center.

Marion lifts her head and looks at me, her eyes just as wide as mine, tears brimming in hers.

I don't realize I'm walking forward until I'm right before her and she reaches toward me, her hand gripping my arm.

"Aqnar…" she breathes.

It worked. It finally worked. I stare at her, believing but not believing at the same time. Everything I wanted. Everything I wished for, is right here in front of me. But she has almost been ripped away from me so many times, I wonder if this is real.

A tear escapes her eye and runs down her cheek.

"Aqnar, I can…I can feel it now. The bond."

I lean closer to her, my gaze searching hers as I run a hand through her hair.

My mate. Even now, right here, she is the most beautiful thing I have ever seen.

"It was my fault," she whispered. "I was the reason it wasn't working all along."

My throat feels tight and unused to speech. "What do you mean?"

She sniffs and glances at the medic who I didn't even notice, too enraptured by the being before me and the feelings she's inciting within me. It is a Glycon male. One of the native descendants of this world. Like a smaller version of an Atari male with translucent blue skin and no fur.

"It appears your mate was implanted with an illegal device. It almost killed her," he says.

I look his way. I can feel the anger simmering beneath all this new emotion. *Something harmed my mate.*

"What?" I almost growl. The medic pales a little.

"This device," he points to something small on a tray by the bed, "was implanted in your mate's reproductive tract. It has been outlawed for contraceptive use by many worlds long ago. I am surprised to even see one that's still working."

"*What?*" I repeat. I understood everything he said but the rage growing within me is preventing me from speaking proper sentences.

"The implant," Marion explains. "They gave me an implant even before I had my first period. It was to prevent any pregnancy and couldn't be removed unless the government granted it. It's never caused a problem before. I didn't...I didn't think it would affect *other* things," she whispers.

"Like our mate bond?"

She nods and gives me a smile that's mixed with both sadness and happiness.

"The device malfunctioned and began to poison your mate's body," the medic continues, and my vision goes red. He begins to speak hurriedly. "Never fear, we have removed the device as you can see, and we applied measures that will kill the infection. It was a good thing you were there at the moment you were. She would have not survived otherwise."

I stare at him, unable to even see him properly with the rage that's consuming me.

"They injected her with something *illegal* that could have *killed* her?" I growl, trying hard to contain the rage rushing through me.

"Well, it seems there was also *external* interference." He says the words like I should care. "Something caused the device to malfunction. We believe your mate's body was trying to reject the device...because of your bond."

Blood drains from my veins.

"*I* did this?" I pull my gaze from the medic to look at Marion.

"Your bite," he explains. "We believe her body has been trying to expel the device unsuccessfully since she was bitten. Biologically, your life spirit would have made her more fertile. This device was a block to that, so it had to be removed."

My eyes grow wide as I stare at my beautiful mate.

"Had it been one of the legal forms of contraception," the medic continues, "it would not have had such an effect."

"My bite almost killed you," I whisper.

She does a sad sort of chuckle. "Gotta try harder than that," she says.

I can't even smile. The heaviness of the situation is too much. Everything that's happened over the past few days is too much.

"Aqnar," Marion's palm presses against my cheek, forcing me to focus on her. "I can feel the bond. I really am yours." Her eyes well up. "That's all that matters."

Hearing her say those words starts a new ache deep in my soul.

"I need to take you home," I say, before glancing toward the medic. I want nothing more than to leave this place and to take her with me, but there is a sliver of doubt. What if, even now, Marion does not want to return with me?

"How soon can she travel?"

He shrugs. "There is no reason she cannot go home now. The medicine is within her system. Even now, the infection is being erased and she will feel no pain."

That's all I need to hear. Pushing the doubt away, I reach down and scoop my mate up into my arms, cradling her to my chest. "Send the bill to my account," I shout over my shoulder as I head back down the corridor.

My mate.

I am holding my mate.

All this time, I had known. But now the bond is pulsing between us. Now the union cannot be denied.

"Heading back to my room?"

I nod. "Where is Klaok?"

In all that's occurred, I forgot he'd helped get me to Marion's room.

"Probably in the closet in my room. He likes the small space and had begun to decorate it as his own."

I snort, bringing her closer to me, warmth slowly filling me.

As I head back down the corridor, I can feel her eyes on me, the silence heavy with unsaid words. Privacy within her quarters does not come soon enough and I kick the door shut behind me as I take my mate to her bed.

Setting her down as gently as I can, I brace my arms above her, as I look down into her face.

She smiles. A soft, almost hesitant smile as she looks back at me. But she is safe now. In my arms.

Like a weight has been lifted from my shoulders, I sag, only barely twisting to the side and taking Marion with me so she ends up on my chest.

"Aqnar?"

"Mm?"

But my lids are already closing, my body's energy reserves at their limit. But at least there is no longer that writhing fear and anxiety that haunted me the last few days.

My mate is here. She is in my arms. And there is nowhere else I'd rather be.

***

Marion

Checking on Klaok in his room, I pad back to the lift and wait patiently as it takes me to the upper level of the house.

Getting back here on our own with an unconscious Aqnar had been a feat. But one call to Aquila and she'd offered her assistance. I am already positive she'll be a great sister-in-law.

For two days, my mate has slept. *My mate.* The thought is still so new and foreign, it sends excited shivers through me.

According to the Rat-Doc, it seems he had not even eaten in the three days that I had gone. Nor had he slept.

It was a miracle that he even had enough strength to be by my side, much less be there at the moment that my stupid implant almost killed me.

He will need sleep and food, and I will be there to nurse him back to health.

Guilt consumes me at the fact he suffered so much, and I have been preparing for when he wakes, stockpiling unperishable food near the bed so I can feed him as soon as his eyes open.

Now, as I pad lightly to the room, wearing one of his soft white shirts, I stop by the doorway.

The dim light makes his skin look like it's glowing softly in the darkness. He is so still, I'm not even sure he is breathing and for the hundredth time, I climb as softly as I can onto the bed and lean close to his nose so I can feel his breath.

The bond pulses. Like a knot of invisible nerves in the center of my chest at every thought of him. His steady heartbeat pulses there too, but the actual feel of his breath gives me comfort.

I'm about to pull away when my wrist is suddenly grabbed. I yelp in surprise, my eyes widening at the same time that Aqnar's golden ones fly open.

"You're awake!" I smile.

His gaze takes a moment to focus and when it lands on me, the undeniable warmth within his eyes sends tingling straight down to my toes.

He inhales deeply, pulling on my wrist so I have no choice but to come closer to him. Immediately, his eyes bleed to black.

The sight of them has an instantaneous effect on the bud nestled within my folds. It throbs and Aqnar inhales once more.

"My ari," he says, pulling me closer.

I chuckle and try to pull away. "You're not well enough for naughty things. You've been asleep for two days and you haven't eaten for five. I don't know how you're not starving."

"I *am* starving." His voice, gravelly from sleep, does nothing but turn me on. "I want to eat."

"Okay, I have food here." I try to stretch away and grab one of the many boxes of food I have had waiting, but Aqnar releases a growl and spins. I'm suddenly on my belly in the center of the bed with him above me.

"Not that," he growls.

"What?"

"That's not what I want to eat."

Realization dawns as he slides down my body and I clench my legs together, my eyes widening. This isn't what I'm meant to be doing with him.

"Marion," he growls. "You have teased me with your scent for the past two days. Three days before that, you denied me of your presence."

"I—" He was aware of me tending to him these past two days? "But you're not well. You need to eat. Let me take care of you."

"I can only think of one thing that will heal me right now." He pulls up the hem of the shirt I wear, exposing my naked ass underneath. I haven't gotten round to buying panties yet and going commando for a short while didn't seem so bad.

Aqnar growls at the sight of me.

"So perfect. More perfect than I remember," he says, his voice going even deeper than before. "And already slick..."

My pussy clenches at his praise and I pant into the bedding.

"Kneel, my precious mate."

At first, I think he wants me to turn and kneel before him, but when he adjusts my body so I'm kneeling while facing away from him, my ass in the air and my face in the bedding, I get a whole new idea of what he wants.

"Good gods," he mutters, his fingers splayed over each ass cheek while his thumbs stroke my slick cunt in the middle. I whimper into the bedding.

"Tell me you feel the bond, Marion. Please tell me that you do."

"Yes," I whimper. It has been pulsing between us ever since that moment the implant was removed, and it has only grown stronger. I don't know what I expected the bond to feel like, but being encased in a constant, warm, comforting glow had not been my expectation.

Now though, that is all I feel. Warmth. Comfort. Love. *Belonging*.

"You are mine, Marion," he growls, his words brushing over my sensitive flesh, and before I can prepare for it, his hot mouth closes over my slickness.

A moan escapes me only to be buried into the bedding as Aqnar forces my ass higher, giving him more access to my cunt.

I scream when he doesn't hesitate and goes full-on to sucking the entire thing into his mouth, his tongue swirling over and through my folds as he moans into my pussy.

With two fingers, he circles my entrance before delving deep as he sucks my clit into his mouth. I scream again, my body shivering. I crash through a peak that comes out of nowhere and, as Aqnar moans at the new flood of juices running into his mouth, I realize something.

The bond. It pulses and grows stronger. I can *feel* Aqnar's moans. Feel the pleasure going through him as if it is my own. It only prolongs the orgasm, making me shudder into the bedding like I'm having a seizure.

"Aqnar, I need…"

"What do you need, my little one?" He still speaks against my pussy, every word vibrating against my clit, sending more love juice flowing through me.

"I need *you*."

The growl that reverberates through the room sounds like it's coming from a powerful animal. Aqnar gives one final hard, long suck before rising behind me. There is little hesitation before I feel the slightly flared tip of his cock press against my softness.

A moan barrels through me and I bite down hard on my bottom lip as I prepare for him. And with one deep moan, Aqnar slides forward.

My eyes roll over with the stretch, my neck tilting back, my eyes going blurry as Aqnar grips my hips and surges forward.

"*Mine*," he growls, seating himself inside me. "Qef me, I can feel you reaching your peak."

I can't speak as another rush of warmth and fever goes through me. My cunt clenches on his shaft, making him roll his hips and slide back before surging forward once more. God, he feels so good.

"I want your everything. Your smiles, your words, your time, your love. Your *cunt*. Everything." Aqnar leans forward, his weight bearing down and pushing me flat onto the bedding.

One arm grips my neck while the other snakes beneath us and finds my clit.

"Fuck!" I scream as his mouth closes over the scar of his mark. "Aqnar."

"My Marion," he growls. I'm not sure if he hears me, he seems possessed, and that only makes me want him more.

"Fuck me," I whisper, and he growls my name one more time. As he begins to piston within me, I lose sense of time and space. All I know is that my mate is here. *My* mate. I have a mate now and a new life and everything I've ever hoped for.

And I couldn't ask for more than that.

By the time Aqnar shudders one last time and collapses to my side, pulling me with him, my body is boneless. Thick slick and spend soak our legs and thighs, the scent of our mating filling the room.

His tongue moves over my neck, and I feel him growing hard again.

"You need rest," I whisper.

His tongue doesn't skip a beat, now moving from my neck down to my shoulder.

"So do you, my mate. I intend to take you again, and again, and again. Till your screams of pleasure are the only thing that ring in my ears."

The bond warms and pulses at his promise.

"But you need food."

"*You* are all I need."

"You haven't been taking care of yourself those past three days." I spin to face him, my words whispering into his chest.

"I needed to find you."

"Why did you come? There was no bond until..."

"Because even if there was no bond, and never would be, I wanted to be with you."

His words hold me captive, and my heart constricts.

"I do not wish to make you weep."

I shake my head and wipe at my eyes. I didn't realize tears were gathering there. "It's good tears," I whisper. "I was so convinced this was all a cruel joke by the universe. That the one male I'd fallen in love with was to be taken away. That I'm not the one for him."

"Never," he growls.

I sniff. "How were you so sure? How were you so sure all along?"

"With or without a bond, I could feel that you are mine. It is stronger even now. I will have no other."

A fresh wave of warmth flows through the bond, filling my soul, warming my flesh.

"Three days without you was too much," he grates.

Some more guilt and sadness fill me at the memory of those three days. "It was torture, but I told myself it was best, for the both of us."

"Never. I will never be without you." He grips my chin gently tilting my face so I'm looking right into those gorgeous eyes. "Tell me you will never leave me again."

I shake my head. "Never." And that is a promise. I don't think I could survive even if I tried.

Resting my head against his chest, I breathe in deep. I've never been more sure of anything than I am about this now.

"Aqnar," I whisper. "I love you."

No words leave his mouth but when a fresh burst of warmth flows through the bond, I know he's feeling exactly what I'm feeling.

"I love you too, my *ari*," he whispers, his head dipping as he kisses into my hair. "Now...I am hungry. Feed me."

I smile. "I thought you'd never ask. I have all this food—"

"Not that," he says, gripping my hips and turning on his back as he lifts me onto his chest. I yelp as he pulls me toward him till his face is nestled between my thighs. "*This*."

I stare at him in surprise as need crashes into me. All I can hear pulsing through me, pulsing through the *bond*, is one word: mine.

I've been claimed by an Atari god. I have found the one place I truly belong.

EPILOGUE

Marion

It's still hard to believe that I live in this house. Even now, looking at my clothes in the wardrobe, I can't believe they're all mine.

I smile, my hand moving to the two marks on my neck. The skin's healed, but the scars haven't disappeared. And they won't.

I don't mind. They're like a wedding ring, of sorts, even though Aqnar went out and bought me an actual ring after reading that humans used to do that. Despite that I told him I don't need one. It's just like the wardrobe filled with clothes and all the other things he's done to make me feel comfortable here.

Leaving the bedroom, I pad to the lift and step on it, waiting patiently as it takes me to the lower level.

Tall green plants complement the white room. Plants from New Earth, ones I've never even seen before. With the smog and bad air on Lower Earth, plants were a thing only the elites had. And now I have more than I can count.

The air is clean and clear. There are no worries...apart from the fact that it's been weeks and Aqnar's friends have not found the other women yet.

Each day that passes, I worry that I may have been the only one who made it out of that nightmare alive.

I startle when strong arms pull me back against a hard chest.

"What brings you sorrow?" Aqnar breathes into my hair. I grin, my shoulders relaxing.

"Just thinking about the other women."

He makes a sound in his throat that's so similar to the sound he makes when his face is buried between my legs. My pussy clenches just at the thought of it and off in the kitchen, Klaok pops his head through the door.

My eyes widen and I dare him to keep his big mouth shut.

My mate is virile. There is no shortage of fucking and if he has even the hint that I am horny, I'll be on my back and pleasured. The way he looks at me, that hunger in his eyes, never dims. I'm the most desired woman on Atar, and he's making sure I know it.

As I glare at Klaok, he smiles at me and disappears again. Aqnar pulls me closer, lifting his hands to my upper arms, one covering my full upper arm, the other covering my nub. He rubs it and kisses my head.

"We will find the other females," he says.

"What makes you so sure?" I sigh, twisting so I'm facing him. "You almost didn't find me."

"But I did, my *ari.*" He smiles, flashing fangs as he runs his tongue over one of them. "The fates are never wrong."

I study him, my eyes narrowing slightly. "What do you mean by that?"

"What I mean—" I screech as he suddenly lifts me into his arms. "Is that I am positive at least one of your friends will be found soon."

My eyes narrow at him. "How do you know?"

"Because, my ari," he leans in, his mouth hovering over mine, "the fates have spoken."

My brows furrow but I don't get to ask anything else as, instead of kissing me, Aqnar's head dips and he swipes his tongue along my neck.

My giggle quickly turns into something else as that roving tongue goes down my collarbone to the valley between my breasts.

Aqnar growls and nuzzles the flesh of one breast. My pussy clenches and just like that, I'm needy again.

There's movement in my peripheral vision as Aqnar heads toward the lift.

"Klaok smells something sweet."

"Klaok!" We both exclaim.

"I'm starting to regret rescuing that damn newot," Aqnar grumbles, before his tongue closes over my nipple.

I gasp into a giggle. "You know you love him."

"Hmm," he growls. "I do. But I love you more, my ari."

AFTERWORD

♥ This concludes Claiming His Mate. ♥

When I first wrote this book, I submitted it to the Claimed Among the Stars Anthology. At first, it was simply a fun project. I did not anticipate that Marion and Aqnar's story would find its way into so many of your hearts!

This extended version was created with lots of love.

I found myself quite admiring Marion. Her fears felt so real, almost as if she were my friend and she was speaking to me. And Aqnar...I felt his pain at the end there. I desperately wanted them to find their way back to each other. (I know it may sound strange since, I am the one writing it, :D. But, while the words come out on paper, I feel every single one of them.)

This is much lighter than my last series—Captured Earth, where the villains really give you a reason to shiver and hide underneath your blanket. If you are looking for something dark and a bit terrifying, you should read that :D.

Thank you so much for reading and as always, lots of love and many blessings!

♥ A.G.

Scan the QR code below if you want to ☞ Join my mailing list, ☞ Find me on Facebook , or ☞ **Join my Patreon (exclusive access NSFW character art, ARCs, quarterly mailouts and more!)**

Craving His Mate

From the moment my fangs began to drip with life spirit, I have known I wanted a mate. One to love. One to care for. *A female all for myself.*

But as the moons pass by, the fates have denied me.

Until I see her.

She is different. She is human. *And she is vulnerable.* More vulnerable than I could have ever imagined.

But she is *mine*. Mine to cherish, mine to keep, and I will do everything in my power to let her know that the moment I laid my eyes on her, she became the reason I breathe.

ALSO BY AGWILDE

Xul: Captured by Aliens Book One

Athena wakes up in hell.

Well…it's an alien slave ship, but it might as well be hell because she only has three choices.

Mate. Become a sex slave. Or be killed.

Great options.

Desperate for freedom, a chance for survival is presented in the hand-some rogue alien called Xul.

But Xul is caught up in problems of his own and a mission he cannot afford to let fail—one that could be easily compromised if he dared open his heart.

That doesn't leave her with many options and it doesn't help that she finds him utterly frustrating...

...and strong, hot, irresistible…

She shouldn't really be thinking about him like that. Should she?

Other books in the series: Crex, Yce, Kyris, Kyro

——

Riv's Sanctuary: Riv's Sanctuary Book One
Abducted from Earth over a year ago, Lauren spent most of that time getting accustomed to her new life as one of the "animals" in an alien zoo.

When she's sold by the zookeeper, her life takes a turn she wasn't expecting. She has no idea where she'll end up till she's brought to a sanctuary owned by a tall blue hunk of an alien called Riv.

Riv's life is quiet and peaceful in a place as far away from civilization as he can manage. So when an annoying chatterbox of a human ends up on his doorstep, he's less than pleased. The human disrupts his life and his solitude and he can't wait to get rid of her.

He's not interested in helping her, and he's definitely not interested in love.

Except…she's managed to wheedle her way in and suddenly those barriers around his heart don't seem so strong anymore.

He has two options: Let her go.

Or let her in.

Other books in the series: Sohut's Protection, Ka'Cit's Haven

——

Ajos: The Restitution Book One
She didn't move to the big city just to be kidnapped by aliens.

That wasn't even possible...

Right?

WRONG.

When Kerena wakes up, she's not on Earth anymore.

Heck, she's not even in the same galaxy, and the face hovering so close she can make out every detail? That face is definitely...not...human.

But before she can really figure out what's going on, Kerena realizes she's caught in the middle of a war—one she was thrust into as soon as she was ripped from Earth.

She's surrounded by aliens in a rebellion, but there's one—the one with the strange golden eyes, minty-teal skin, and rippling muscles—that holds her attention.

His presence is magnetic and his heated gaze makes something stir deep within her.

He's battling something that has nothing to do with the war and his warning that she should stay away does not go unheeded.

He's a dangerous rebel fighter. She gets that. So...why is he still hovering so close? And why is he growling at everyone that so much as looks in her direction?

Most of all, why does he keep looking at her like she belongs to ... HIM?

———

Arrival: Captured Earth Book One

ADIRA

The machines came, and they trampled us all.

I have nothing left. No family. No friends. No home.

They harvest us. They breed us. They feed from us…

There is no hope…Not until one fateful moment when my eyes open and I see something streaking across the skies.

What appears is like a demon before my eyes…

But can they be worse than the evil already upon us?

I will just have to wait and see.

FER'RO

Sailing across the stars for what feels like eons…we have followed our enemy to a little blue planet.

We had wanted to arrive before them…now I think we may be too late.
But when we kill the first Scrit and I see the being drowning within its depths, I know I have to save it.
And *it*…turns out to be a *her*. **A female.**
This planet has hope yet. I will save her and her kind.
…Little do I know…she's the one who ends up saving me instead.

Dark. Steamy. Gritty. A thrilling romance intertwined in a plot that will give you chills.

Other books in the series: Base Zero, Cataclysm, War

———

Scan the QR code to view all books

ABOUT THE AUTHOR

A. G. Wilde is an avid reader, a gamer, a lover of all things space, alien, and sci-fi.

She is addicted to intense romance, irresistible heroes, and deliciously naughty things.

|● patreon.com/agwilde
facebook.com/agwilde
twitter.com/authoragwilde
instagram.com/authoragwilde
amazon.com/author/agwilde

www.ingramcontent.com/pod-product-compliance
Lightning Source LLC
Chambersburg PA
CBHW030756190726
48285CB00003B/885